"You made your demands, Daniela. Now I have made mine."

"Your terms being the immediate announcement of a fake engagement?" She was incredulous, her chest rising and falling with outrage.

"Not just an engagement." He turned to face her, noticing once again how much warmth her eyes held. He could almost feel the heat emanating from her, along with that intoxicating scent she wore. The galloping of his heart seemed to slow when he considered the deep golden-brown depths of her eyes.

"You will be my wife."

As he spoke the words and saw the shock turn to anger in her eyes, he felt a strange calm settle within him. He had known for six months that it might come to this. He had known that she would fight him every step of the way. And now, seeing her ablaze with fury and outrage, he thought maybe she would withstand the burden of being tied to him. He had to believe that. He had no other choice.

Amanda Cinelli

—

THE VOWS HE MUST KEEP

HARLEQUIN
PRESENTS

Recycling programs
for this product may
not exist in your area.

ISBN-13: 978-1-335-89419-9

The Vows He Must Keep

Harlequin Enterprises ULC
22 Adelaide St. West, 40th Floor
Toronto, Ontario M5H 4E3, Canada
www.Harlequin.com

Printed in U.S.A.

Amanda Cinelli was born into a large Irish Italian family and raised in the leafy green suburbs of County Dublin, Ireland. After dabbling in a few different career paths, she finally found her calling as an author after winning an online writing competiton with her first finished novel. With three small daughters at home, she usually spends her days doing school runs, changing diapers and writing romance. She still considers herself unbelievably lucky to be able to call this her day job.

Books by Amanda Cinelli

Harlequin Presents

Resisting the Sicilian Playboy

Secret Heirs of Billionaires

The Secret to Marrying Marchesi

Monteverre Marriages

One Night with the Forbidden Princess
Claiming His Replacement Queen

Visit the Author Profile page
at Harlequin.com for more titles.

For Keith, the hero of my own love story.

CHAPTER ONE

VALERIO MARCHESI AWOKE to the thunder of his own heartbeat, his senses taking in the complete darkness that surrounded him and the feeling of cold sweat on his skin. It was not the first time he had awoken in a state of panic in the past six months. His physician had called it post-traumatic stress, and like countless others had sympathised with him for his ordeal. He didn't want their damn sympathy.

Gritting his teeth, he fought through the fog left by the entire bottle of whisky he had downed the night before and reminded himself why he'd completely sworn off drinking in re-cent months. As he came fully to consciousness and tried to sit up, he became instantly aware of two things.

One, judging by the soft clearing of a throat nearby, he was not alone in the room. And two, he couldn't move his upper body because he had been tied to his own bed.

Any remaining effect of the alcohol in his system instantly evaporated. The room was dark, but he could just about make out the blurry outline of his luxury yacht's master cabin around him. Both of his wrists had been tied to the ornate wooden headboard on either side of his head, using what felt like soft fabric. He tested the bonds, black panic snaking up his back like wildfire, followed by the swift kick of fury.

He would die before he allowed this to happen again.

'Good, you're awake.'

A female voice cut across the shadows.

'I was just debating if I should throw some water over your head.'

The woman's voice silenced his growls momentarily as his brain scrambled to differentiate between the danger of his past and in the present moment. Drawing on some recent meditative practice, he inhaled deeply past the adrenaline, focusing his mind to a fine point. The woman's voice sounded familiar, but Valerio couldn't quite place it other than to note that it was English, upper class, and deathly calm. Nothing like the rough-hewn criminals from his memories, but one never knew.

'What the hell is going on here?' he demanded gruffly. 'Show your face.'

Heels tapped across the wooden floor, the

dim light from the curtain-covered windows throwing her shape into relief. She was tall, for a woman, and had the kind of exaggerated full-figured curves that made his spine snap to attention. A knot of awareness tightened in his abdomen, catching him completely by surprise. At thirty-three years of age, he'd believed himself long past the kind of embarrassing loss of control usually attributed to youth. But it seemed he hadn't been around a woman in so long, apparently *anyone* was going to ignite his starving libido. Even someone who was possibly attempting to hold him hostage.

It was a strange kind of twist, considering his most recent brush with captivity had been the catalyst for his self-imposed isolation from society. Had his broken mind moved on to finding some kind of thrill in the possibility of danger?

He pulled at the headboard once again, a sharp hiss escaping his lips at the burn of the fabric on his skin. The sheet that only partially covered his nude body slipped further down the bed.

'You're only going to hurt yourself by struggling.'

'Well, then, cut these damn ropes off,' he growled, trying and failing to keep the edge from his voice. 'I don't keep money here, if that's what you are after.'

A soft laugh sounded out, closer this time. 'I'm not here to rob you, Marchesi. The ropes are for my own safety, considering the night we've just had.'

'Your safety...?' He tried and failed to process her words, feeling the tug of a memory in his mind.

He knew that voice.

Soft hands brushed against his skin as the woman gently adjusted the sheet over his body. Another shiver of awareness heated him from the inside out. It had been so damn long...and her familiar scent was all around him, tugging at those memories. He breathed her in greedily, feeling the warm blend of sweetness and musk penetrate his chest, melting some of the ice that seemed permanently lodged inside.

A soft lamp was flicked on beside the bed without warning, the sudden golden light making him wince with pain. The woman came into focus slowly, a watercolour of long ebony curls and flawless dark caramel skin. Recognition hit him with a sudden jolt, his eyes narrowing, and all anxiety was suddenly replaced by swift, unbridled anger.

'Dani.'

'Only my friends get to call me that, Marchesi.'

Daniela Avelar narrowed her eyes, pulling

a chair closer to the bed and lowering herself down elegantly, as though sitting down to afternoon tea.

'You made it clear the last time I saw you that you are *not* my friend.'

Guilt hit him in the gut even as he fought to remain outraged. Memories assailed him of the last time they had spoken. Six months ago he had delivered the most painful speech of his life, marking the death of his business partner at a memorial ceremony. His best friend. Her twin brother.

Duarte Avelar had been shot dead right in front of him, after they'd both been taken hostage after an event in Rio de Janeiro and kept at gunpoint for two weeks, deep in the slums of the city. The story had made global news. He'd been lamented as a hero for surviving. He alone knew the truth of what had happened.

He had forced himself to hold it together throughout his friend's memorial service on a rainy morning in the English countryside. He had tried to speak words that would honour the sacrifice Duarte had made to save his life. But eventually he'd lost his grip on control and had torn out of the church as if the fires of hell had been at his heels, needing to get away from all the sympathetic stares and unbearable grief.

But Dani had run after him, standing in front

of the door of his chauffeur-driven car. Daniela
Avelar—a woman who prided herself on being
one of the best PR and marketing strategists in
the business, and who had always seemed to
look down her nose at him and his wild playboy lifestyle. She was a woman who never asked
anyone for help, not even her own brother, but
she had begged him to stay. She'd held on to his
arm and begged him to tell her the truth of what
had happened in Brazil...to let her help him.

He had scraped together enough composure to growl at her, telling her that knowing wouldn't make anything different. That it
wouldn't bring Duarte back. Then he had got
into his car and driven away, pretending not to
be affected by the sight of the tears streaming
down her cheeks.

Shame was a familiar lead weight in his solar
plexus even now.

In the lamplit room, Daniela crossed her legs,
drawing his attention to the spindly-heeled
shoes on her feet. She had been working for
Velamar as their PR strategist for years, so he
was used to her trademark pinstriped trousers
and perfectly pressed blouses, with their delicate
ribbons tied at the throat. But on this cream-
coloured confection the collar was undone, the
ribbons hanging limp and creased as though

someone had grabbed them and held them tight in their grip.

She looked tired, though she was trying hard not to let it show. But he could see the faint dark shadows under her eyes, the tightness around her mouth. He wondered if grief had stolen her perfect polished image and grace, just as it had stolen his carefree nonchalance.

'Do you have any idea how long I've been trying to find you?' She met his eyes without fear or hesitation—an easy feat considering she had him half naked and trussed to a bed.

'I'll admit that of all the ways you could have got my attention this is quite creative, if not a little insensitive.' He spoke easily, pulling at the bonds and feeling them slide slightly to one side. The knots were strong, but not strong enough. She might be about to inherit part-ownership of Velamar—one of the most exclusive yacht charter companies in the world—but she was no sailor.

Valerio ignored the pull in his chest at the thought of the brand he had built from the ground up, the work that had once given him purpose and pride. 'Did you ever think that maybe I didn't want to be found?'

'You walked away from your responsibilities, Marchesi.'

'My company is in good hands.'

'*Our* company is in brilliant hands—considering I've been running it alone for six months.'

She sat and surveyed him like a queen on her throne, which was not inaccurate considering the Avelar family name was practically royalty in their native Brazil.

'But your employees don't respond to my own particular brand of authority, it seems. They're practically begging for the return of their playboy CEO and his infamous parties.'

'Final warning. Untie me and get the hell off my yacht, Daniela.'

'You don't remember anything about last night, do you?' She raised one brow, watching him with curiosity and the faintest ghost of a smile.

Valerio looked around the room once more, the pain in his head sharpening. The last thing he remembered was storming out of his brother's sprawling villa in Tuscany after an embarrassing display of temper and popping open the first alcoholic beverage he could find. He'd drunk alone and brooded silently in the back of his chauffeur-driven car the entire way to where his yacht had been moored in nearby Genoa.

He'd always known that yesterday would be a difficult day, considering he'd avoided his family for so long, but he'd thought he'd done enough work on himself to get through a couple of hours in their company. He had expected pity and tiptoeing around him. He hadn't been prepared for their anger. Their judgement. They didn't know anything about what he'd gone through...what he'd done. All they cared about was the precious Marchesi image and the worrying rumours that he'd gone insane.

His rages were unpredictable, and tended to fog his memory, so he didn't remember much. But he was pretty sure he had smashed a few of his brother's expensive vases on his way out.

Wincing, he tried to sit up more fully against the wooden headboard, only managing a couple of inches before he inhaled sharply against the sudden throb of pain that assaulted his cranium. What had been in that whisky?

'Don't move too fast. The doctor gave you a mild sedative.'

'You *drugged* me?'

'You tried to take on my entire security team one by one. You were in some kind of a trance. We couldn't...' She swallowed hard. 'You weren't yourself.'

Growling, he pulled hard against the bonds once more. A satisfying creak sounded from the wooden beam above him. He saw the first glimmer of unease flicker in her eyes.

'This was the only way I could think of to make you listen.' She stood up, her eyes darting to the door at the opposite side of the room. 'I didn't mean for it to go this far... I didn't think you were as out of control as your brother said.'

'You spoke to Rigo?' His brother—the damn idiot. He had promised Valerio that if he accepted the invitation he would keep his appearance in Tuscany to himself. But then, Valerio hadn't planned on causing such a scene. Once again, he'd lived up to his reputation of being the reckless wild-card Marchesi brother.

The shame burned his gut.

Daniela cleared her throat. 'Look, I've been patient. I've given you more than enough time, considering what happened, but now it's time for you to come back. The board members are not happy with my choices as acting CEO. There's a motion in place to sell off my brother's design projects and pull out of a large chunk of our charity commitments, and I'm the only one blocking their way.' She pinched the bridge of her nose, a deep sigh escaping her chest. 'This kind of unrest is bad news. With the pressure of the new *Sirinetta* launch coming up, I just don't have time for it.'

Her words rang in his mind, fuelling his anger and disbelief. Nettuno Design was Duarte's brainchild—an offshoot of the Velamar brand—and the maritime engineering firm had created the very first *Sirinetta* mega-yacht. It was the yacht that had launched their modest luxury yacht charter firm right up into the upper echelons of society five years ago. It had been the catalyst that had brought them in contact with figures of royalty and power across the globe, and wealth beyond their dreams.

'So you decided to kidnap me to tell me this?'

She narrowed her eyes on him with barely restrained irritation. 'A second meeting is being held the day after tomorrow in Monte Carlo, with more board members flying in. I have information that they are planning to vote me out.' She took a deep breath, meeting his eyes. 'I need your help. I need you to get over whatever this is and come back.'

'I know it's not technically official, but *I* named you acting CEO in place of both me and Duarte,' he gritted out, his friend's name sounding wooden and unfamiliar in his mouth. 'They can't vote you out. They're bluffing.'

'Considering Duarte is about to be declared legally dead, and what with all the recent rumours in the press about your mental instability… I'm afraid they can.'

Valerio froze, the news sending his blood cold.

Duarte's official death certificate had not been issued—he'd made sure of it. As executor of the estate, he'd specifically given the authorities more time before Daniela could legally inherit all her brother's assets.

And now she dared to barge on to *his* yacht and calmly make demands while she was sitting on a bombshell of this magnitude? *Dio*, she had no idea what this meant.

Oblivious, she continued. 'Apart from the fact that our reputation is being pulled under the proverbial bus…they know I'm not qualified. I mean, to be honest, I know it too. I'm a PR strategist—not a leader or a figurehead. I've never done this before.'

'Let me free,' he growled.

'Not until you agree to come to the meeting.'

She folded her arms under her breasts, the movement pushing up her ample cleavage and making the blood roar in his ears.

'Daniela… I'm warning you. You have no idea what's going on here, so let me off this bed right now.'

'I'm quite aware of what's going on in my own company. *You're* the one who's been MIA for months on end, and I can't risk you disappearing on me again.' She closed her eyes briefly, opening them to lock on his with intent. 'I don't care if you hate me for this. I will do whatever it takes to save my brother's legacy.'

She claimed that *he* was the only one who could save the company? The man she had once called a frivolous playboy? She had no idea what he had been uncovering over the past six months. Hell, he wasn't even sure *he* knew.

What he did know was that she wasn't the only one prepared to do whatever it took to save something. But the person he'd been trying to save seemed intent on putting herself in danger, again and again.

Anger gave him an extra spurt of energy, and the last knot that bound his wrists slipped free.

Like a coiled spring, Valerio launched himself off the bed.

Dani felt a shocked scream rise in her throat but she refused to let it free—refused to believe that this man whom she had known for almost half of her thirty-one years on the earth would ever actually harm her.

But this was not the Valerio she had watched from afar—the playboy reprobate who'd bedded half the socialites in Europe and charmed everyone he met with his pirate's smile and his wild thirst for adventure. It was as though any trace of light in his deep blue eyes had been snuffed out.

Before she had a chance to run, he had grabbed her by the wrists to stop her. He pulled her to face him but she shoved him back, the movement accidentally sending them both tumbling down onto the bed, with her body landing directly on top of his.

Large hands moved to grip her waist and she inhaled sharply at the feel of his skin as it seemed to burn through the fabric of her shirt. She shifted position, trying to stand, but her movements somehow only served to press her even harder against him.

'*Dio*, stay still,' he cursed, his voice sounding strangled and raw.

It seemed a lifetime ago that Dani had fantasised about exactly this kind of situation. Her foolish teenage self had once dreamed of having Valerio Marchesi look at *her* the way she had seen him look at a parade of beauties, while she'd watched awkwardly from the sidelines. But he had long ago made it clear that there was no way he would ever look at her as anything but his best friend's chubby, boring, know-it-all twin sister. The annoying third wheel to their perfect partnership.

No, there was nothing sexual that she could see in the barely controlled fury glittering in his eyes now, as he stared up at her. He seemed to inhale deeply as her hair fell over her shoulder, forming a cocoon of ebony curls around them. His hands flexed just underneath her ribcage, his eyes lowering to where the buttons on her blouse had come undone, revealing the far too large breasts threatening to spill over the plain white lace of her sensible bra. And still his hands tightened, holding her still and stopping her retreat.

'Let go of me. What do you think you're doing?'

She was furious, her knees moving directly towards the part of him where she could cause the most damage. Not that she *wanted* to hurt him, but he was being completely unreasonable—and she refused to accept that she had lost the upper hand now, after all her careful planning, simply because he had more brute strength.

He easily controlled her, pinning her legs with his own and pulling her arms directly above her head.

'What do *I* think I'm doing?' He repeated her question, a harsh bark of laughter erupting from his chest as he grabbed both her wrists and tied them to the headboard he had just freed himself from. 'I believe there is an English expression… Turnabout is fair play?'

Dani was breathing heavily with the exertion of trying to fight him. She didn't see his plan until she was already tied in place. Disbelief turned quickly to anger as she tried and failed to pull herself free.

'Thrashing around like that really isn't going

to help either of us. Especially considering our position and my lack of clothing.'

Dani became completely still, looking down to where their bodies were melded together. Her legs in the dark wool of her designer trousers were wrapped around the bare skin of his torso. She felt her cheeks heat up, perspiration beading on the back of her neck. He said he was unaffected, and yet just a moment ago she had moved her hips and she could have sworn she'd felt...

Suddenly he moved. With an impressive flex of muscle, he slid his large body out from underneath her with surprising ease, gently laying her down on the pillows before moving out of her vision.

'I understand that you have some anger towards me...' His voice sounded husky, and he was slightly out of breath from his exertions in freeing himself. 'But, whatever this game was tonight, know that it was out of line.'

'I'm not playing a game. I told you that I had to have you restrained for your own safety and mine. You were threatening to kill your own bodyguard, for goodness' sake, and we couldn't snap you out of it.'

She tried to lift her head to look at him, but on seeing a flash of tall, naked male, she returned her head to the pillows with a thump.

'Maybe so. But you're trying to manipulate me. To force my hand. Maybe in the past I might have seen the humour in all this…but I am not that man any more.'

'Where are you going?' she asked innocently, remembering that while she might have temporarily lost the upper hand in this battle, she was far from losing the war.

'I am going to walk out of here and leave you to think about your actions for a while.'

He flicked on the full lights in the room and she watched as he walked towards the doorway, then suddenly stood still. Her body tensed in the long silence, and she imagined the look on his face as he realised his mistake. Because they were not on his luxury yacht in Genoa. They weren't even on Italian soil.

He let out a dark curse in Italian and Dani felt an unruly smile threaten at the corner of her lips. She listened as his footsteps boomed across the luxury wooden floor of the cabin and out into the hallway.

He might not remember the events of last night but she did—with painful clarity. She remembered having Valerio's own personal bodyguard help her carry his boss onto the brand-new, not officially launched *Sirinetta II* mega-yacht that she'd commandeered, and then sending the man on a fool's errand to the doc-

tor in town so that she could order the captain
to sail off into the night.

She waited for Valerio to return, realising that
it was impossible even to attempt to look lady-
like while she was sprawled face-down on a
bed, her arms pinned at an awkward upwards
angle as they were.

'Where the *hell* have you brought me?'

His voice suddenly boomed from the other
side of the room and the door of the cabin
banged open on its hinges, making her jump.

'Back so soon? I've had barely four minutes
of my time out. Hardly enough time to think
about my actions.'

He came to a stop beside the bed. Dani turned
her head on the pillow and allowed her eyes to
travel up his impressive form. Mercifully he had
donned the clothing she had grabbed from his
yacht's cabin during their swift exit. The dark
blue jeans fitted him perfectly and the plain
black T-shirt was like a second skin, mould-
ing to his impressive biceps. The rumours of
his mental state were yet to be confirmed, but
he certainly hadn't stopped working on his infamous abs since he'd gone into exile, that was
for sure. If anything, he'd kicked it up a notch.

'I'd say we're cruising somewhere near Cor-
sica.' She met his intense gaze without showing her unease. 'I decided to multitask and give

you a tour of the new model while we discussed our approach for this meeting. And before you get any ideas, the wheelhouse is locked down and the captain has been ordered to refuse entry without my passcode. Company policy.'

'You...' He took a step away, pinching the bridge of his nose. 'You had me drugged and loaded onto one of my own company's yachts. And then you turned my own crew against me?'

'*Our* crew.' She smiled sweetly. 'You forget that I've got quite familiar with all the staff in our employ over the past six months, *partner*.'

'Order them back to land. Now.'

He leaned over her, one hand braced on the headboard beside her. His breath fanned her ear, sending gooseflesh down her neck. Evidently being tied up and ordered about was something her inner self got a dark thrill out of, regardless of the fact that the man giving those orders was a selfish bastard who had abandoned her when she'd needed him most.

No, she corrected herself, he had abandoned *his company*. The company that *she* was going to inherit half of once her brother's estate was released, as well as countless other assets and properties—thanks to his death. And that was without the inheritance she'd already got after their parents' accidental deaths seven years before.

If she had still been the praying kind, she

would have thought that someone somewhere up above had really taken a dislike to the Avelar family. But she no longer believed in anything but cold hard facts, and right now keeping her brother's prized Nettuno Design a part of the company was what she needed to focus on.

Valerio and Duarte had had countless other investments, but they had spent twelve years building Velamar from the ground up. Was he just going to sit back and allow his work to be poached by the vultures? Not on *her* watch.

'You can leave me tied up here as long as you like. I won't make the order.' She flexed her fingers, feeling a slight numbness creeping in from her position.

'Dani—'

'I told you not to call me that,' she snapped. 'Use my proper name. You and I are business partners now and nothing more.'

'Do business partners usually tie each other up naked and watch from the shadows?'

'I wasn't watching you.' She bristled, hating the way that her skin immediately turned to gooseflesh at his words and hating the sinfully erotic image they created. She closed her eyes, praying he couldn't see. That he didn't notice the ridiculous effect he still had on her, no matter how much she'd believed she'd got past it.

'It's pretty clear that you were sitting there in

the dark, waiting for me to wake up. What were you thinking about all that time, Daniela? The company? Or was there a small part of you that enjoyed having me at your mercy?'

He crouched low, sliding a lock of hair from her face, and waited until she met his gaze. Dani swallowed hard, fighting the urge to lick her suddenly dry lips.

'You shouldn't have followed me. You could have just emailed me the details of the meeting. But you didn't trust me to show up, did you? Bastard that I am...' He let his fingers trail along her face, smoothing her hair behind her ear. 'You found me and saw me at my worst. The runaway playboy, the raging madman in the flesh. Tell me that you didn't relish the opportunity to punish me, to ensure I didn't have an easy escape. Tell me you didn't enjoy it, Daniela.'

She bit her lower lip, knowing that he was just playing a game. Trying to make her uncomfortable enough to make her order the yacht back to land and let him cut his responsibilities all over again.

She turned her face, opening her eyes to meet his directly and summoning all the strength she had. 'There is nothing enjoyable about watching you give up and walk away from everything you've worked so hard to achieve,' she said boldly. 'You could have died in Rio too, but you didn't. I thought that might have made you see life as more precious than you did before, that you might take things more seriously. But you've just been running away, pretending that nothing's happened.'

Valerio's hand dropped as though she had burned him. In a way, she supposed she had. Guilt momentarily pulled at her subconscious, but she pushed it away, knowing that she was doing what she needed to do. Lucky for her, she knew exactly what to say to keep Valerio Marchesi at a distance in order to protect herself. She always had. But right now she needed him on her side more than she needed him to get away from her.

She felt his hands on hers as he silently loosened the ropes at her wrists. She worked herself free as quickly as she could, noting that his knots were skilled. He had been a sailor practically from birth, after all. The blood rushed quickly back into her hands as she sat up, rubbing at her wrists, and saw that he had moved to the other side of the room. He stood completely still, looking out of the window to the blackness beyond. There was no moon tonight—nothing to light their way in the night. Only dark clouds and the subtle sheen of the waves that surrounded them.

'I know all too well how precious life is, Daniela. If you think I've been running away, then you really don't know me at all.' Valerio's voice was cold and distant, bleak. 'If you think that I could ever hope to forget what happened... If you think I haven't gone over and over every single second...' He shook his head as he turned to face her, and a look of complete darkness seemed to cast a shadow over him.

Dani felt emotion burn her throat. She wished she could take her words back but knew it was done. Since Valerio had left her alone at Duarte's funeral all those months ago, she had been filled with a rage of her own. *He* had been the one to return from their trip alive after weeks of being presumed dead. *He* had been the one to refuse to tell her the full details of what had happened, only revealing that Duarte had been killed shortly before Valerio had escaped.

Her twin had been murdered and she'd had no idea. There had been no sudden shift in the cosmos, no supernatural feeling of loss or pain. Instead she had felt nothing. And that feeling of disconnected numbness had continued for the past six months as she had thrown herself into keeping the company running smoothly.

'I'm sorry. I didn't mean to be so harsh.' She breathed past the emotion in her throat, wishing she'd chosen her words more carefully. 'But it doesn't help that I don't know anything about what happened other than—'

'It doesn't matter.' He cut across her, pure steel in his voice. 'I'll be there at the meeting. I'll say whatever you want me to say.'

'You will?' She paused, struggling to make sense of his sudden shift from outraged to passive. Yes, her words had been harsh, but…

'I will come to Monte Carlo with you because it's what Duarte would want.' He took a step forward. 'But in return I need you to do something for me.'

'You're giving *me* terms?' She tilted her head. 'I should have known there would be a catch.'

He folded his arms across his chest in a pose filled with dominance and attitude, but his voice quavered slightly as he spoke. 'I have one condition, yes, and I need you to trust me that it's necessary and non-negotiable.'

'Is this a security thing?' She took in the tension in his posture, the way his fists were pulled tight by his sides. 'I have taken on board all the terms you laid down with that crazy security team before you disappeared. I never go anywhere without their protection.'

'You think I haven't been checking in over the past six months?' He shook his head, his voice deepening with some unknown emotion. 'I may not have been here, but I didn't run away.

I need you to understand that. There were things I had to do before I could…' He frowned, turning slightly to look out across the murky water through the window. When he began speaking again, his voice was deeper. 'When we realised things were going to end badly in Rio… I made a promise to him that if I survived I would keep you safe.'

Dani felt a lump in her throat, but pushed it away, reminding herself that getting emotional would only put her in a vulnerable position. He wanted her to trust him? Valerio hadn't even tried to keep whatever promises he'd made—he had blocked her out and walked away at his earliest convenience, preferring to process his grief alone. Or more likely in the company of expensive whisky and a string of beautiful women across the globe.

She had learned the hard way that she could only rely on herself. Folding her arms tightly across her chest, she didn't bother to hide the ice that crept into her voice. 'Just outline your terms, Marchesi.'

His jaw flexed menacingly, and a hardness entered his gaze as they stood toe to toe in the darkness of the master cabin. When he finally spoke, the huskiness was gone from his voice and had been replaced by a hint of that sultry charm she remembered.

'The board believe that Velamar is weakened because of my absence…that I am unreliable and unstable. If you want my presence to be of any benefit, then we need to show them a better angle. If I get off this yacht tomorrow, my only term is that you stay by my side. That we stand together as a couple.'

'Of course. I'm the PR guru here. I can find a good spin for all this, if that's what you're worried about.'

She frowned at his use of the word 'couple'— a strange expression for their partnership. Still, she forced a smile, hardly believing the upward turn this venture had taken. An hour ago she had been terrified of what he might do after her actions tonight. She had taken a risk, forcing his hand this way. For now, she was happy to have him firmly on the side of the company and getting his mind back into the game.

'I presumed you would be more averse to the idea of us being together.' Valerio raised one dark brow, shrugging a shoulder as he moved to open the door. 'It's settled, then. We will announce our engagement first thing in the morning.'

blind wood design. He knew from memory that
the quietest smooth surfaces were an illusion,
and in fact filled with discreet touch buttons
and modern technological gadgets.

"What did you just say?"

Daniela's voice was low and tentative, and
her flashing amber eyes filled with disbelief as
he looked over his shoulder.

CHAPTER TWO

VALERIO MOVED AWAY from Daniela's frozen form
and walked quickly down the hallway. A part
of him longed to turn around and reveal the
full truth of their situation—the real reason he
had promised to keep her safe, the truth behind
his disappearance from society and the reason
it needed to be this way. He had told himself
he was biding his time, gathering all his facts.
He hadn't expected the imminent issue of Duarte's death certificate to completely force his
hand this way.

He focused on some deep and steady breaths
as he emerged into the open-plan living space
of the yacht's accommodation deck.

He remembered attending the initial meetings for the *Sirinetta II* just before they'd left
on their trip to South America. It had been one
of Duarte's most innovative design projects yet.
His senses felt overloaded by the bright and airy
interior, with its open-plan spaces and natural

blond wood design. He knew from memory that the endless smooth surfaces were an illusion, and in fact filled with discreet touch cabinets and modern technological gadgets.

'What did you just say?'

Daniela's voice had risen an entire octave, and her flashing amber eyes filled with disbelief as he looked over his shoulder.

Her cheeks were flushed with the warmth of the force of her anger at his proposal. Well, technically he hadn't proposed so much as *declared* their engagement… He winced inwardly. Probably not the best way he could have done things.

Turning away from her, he touched a panel and grabbed a bottle of water from one of the discreet built-in fridges that slid out from behind the wood. 'We can make the announcement in the morning papers if you get on it now. You are the PR guru, as you said. I assume you have contacts who can word it to make it all appear as romantic as possible.'

'Valerio, we are *business* partners—our alliance is solid enough without turning it into some kind of media circus.'

'Did you or did you not say that rumours surrounding my disappearance from the public eye have cast doubt on my stability?'

'I—I am experienced with appeasing doubt.' She stammered a little over her words. 'It's been my job to control Velamar's public image for the past seven years and I'm quite good at it without resorting to outright lies and…and pageantry!'

'My terms are that we release the news that we are engaged. That is non-negotiable.'

He took a long drink of water, trying to shake off the feeling of adrenaline still running riot in his veins. He was always like this after a bad night—he felt on edge for days. But now, knowing that someone had pushed to have Duarte declared legally dead even when he had made every effort to hold it off… He had to act now. He had to be ready.

Dani was silent for a long time, a frown marring her brow as she shook her head slowly from side to side. 'I don't buy it. What aren't you telling me?'

Valerio walked out onto the open-air deck, gritting his teeth at the sound of her heels as she instantly followed him. Of *course* she wouldn't just meekly accept his terms and move forward; this was Dani, after all.

He closed his eyes and inhaled a deep breath of cold sea air into his lungs. He wasn't ready for this—for any of it. He needed to get off this yacht and find some breathing room while he built himself up to step back into his old life. Daniela thought she knew everything he had been doing for the past six months. Yes, he was broken, but not in the way that she thought. Despite public opinion, he was far from losing his mind. He had never had a more single-minded focus.

But that focus was entirely set on revenge.

'Valerio…' She appeared at his side, her expression a mixture of confusion and concern. 'Talk to me. Please.'

She believed him to be mad… Let her think that. Maybe then he would be able to shield her from the true monster he had become. Before all this he had been a good man. He might even have deserved a woman like her. Not that he had ever truly considered having her. He had always known she was off-limits to him. His friendship with Duarte had been worth more to him than any pleasure he might have got from pursuing any inconvenient attraction he may or may not have had. She was and would always be his best friend's sister.

Untouchable.

Now he was just the man who had let her down in so many ways. He'd known that she disliked him before, but now that he'd abandoned her to run Velamar for months without explanation… It was his own fault if she hated him, and perhaps that was a blessing in disguise. The man who stood beside her right now was nothing but darkness and regret. If hating him would keep her safe from getting too close, he'd bear every moment of the burn from her wrath.

He turned away from her, bracing his hands on the railing and looking down at the inky foam of the midnight waves as they crashed along the side of the yacht.

'You made your demands, Daniela. Now I have made mine. I'm willing to forgive your actions tonight so long as you agree to my terms without any further questioning.'

'Your terms being the immediate announcement of a fake engagement?' She was incredulous, her chest rising and falling with outrage.

'Not just an engagement.' He turned to face her, noticing once again how much warmth her eyes held. He could almost feel the heat emanating from her, along with that intoxicating scent she wore. The galloping of his heart seemed to slow when he considered the deep golden-brown depths of her eyes.

'You will be my wife.'

As he spoke the words and saw the shock turn to anger in her eyes, he felt a strange calm settle within him. He had known for six months that it might come to this. He had known that she would fight him every step of the way. And now, seeing her ablaze with fury and outrage, he thought maybe she would withstand the burden of being tied to him. He had to believe that. He had no other choice.

Dani stood frozen, her mouth refusing to form words, as Valerio took a step forward.

'A long time ago Duarte told me to keep the hell away from you unless I planned to marry you.' Valerio shook his head, looking out at the darkness that surrounded them. 'I doubt he ever thought things would come to this.'

'This is ridiculous.'

Dani turned and walked inside, needing to move away from him. He had no idea what he was saying. How hurtful it was on so many levels. Even when she'd moved back to London and become engaged to another man, she'd fought not to let herself think of him. She growled in her throat, marching into the living area and reaching for her laptop—only for a large male hand to close over hers, stopping her.

'Valerio, stop. Let me show you my plans and we can discuss this rationally.'

'Your brother knew the kind of guy I am. He knew the perfect way to ensure I would never touch you.'

'You never *wanted* to touch me!' She practically growled it. She felt heat rise into her cheeks at her own words...at the hint of years of hidden feelings under the surface.

He opened his mouth as if to speak, then paused. For a moment there was nothing but weighted silence between them and the sound of the waves outside the open door.

Valerio cleared his throat, waited until she met his eyes. 'The day before Duarte was killed, we planned an escape. He told me that if anything happened to him and I survived, I was to keep you close. To give you my name and protect you.'

'I don't need a husband for protection. That is *my* choice. Not his.'

Dani fought against the lump of emotion that tightened in her throat at the thought of her brother instructing his best friend to care for her. He must have known that she would never agree to this kind of archaic showing of duty, or whatever it was.

Valerio turned away briefly, pushing his hands through his hair. 'I swore to him. I promised that I would follow his wishes. And I spent the last six months…'

Dani looked up at him, seeing a strange look in his eyes. 'You spent six months…what? Trying to find a way out of it? *That's* what it was all about?'

'No…you don't understand.'

'I think I understand far more than you do, Marchesi.' She picked up a small bag from under the desk and threw it onto the low sofa between them. 'I'm done here. I apologise for wasting your time tonight. Believe when I say I wish I hadn't bothered. The code for the wheelhouse is in that bag, along with your mobile phone. Order the Captain to take you wherever you need, so long as you're off this yacht by morning.'

'This won't just disappear because you order me away. I'm coming to Monte Carlo. You say you need me for this board meeting, so I'll be there.'

'I'll find another way. I always do.' She fought to keep her voice level, to hide her hurt and anger under the professional veil she wore so well. 'Pretend tonight never happened. Consider yourself officially relieved of your duties to Velamar. To me. All of them.'

She didn't wait for his response before she walked away, not stopping to take a breath until she had her cabin door firmly closed between them and she was sure that he hadn't followed her.

Then she closed her eyes tight and sank back against the door, allowing herself a single moment to feel the blinding pain of knowing how little Valerio Marchesi had ever cared about her.

'I can't believe you didn't take a photograph. I'd pay good money to see either one of the

Marchesi brothers all tied up.' Hermione Hall waggled her brows seductively from across the terrace table of their favourite little Monte Carlo café.

Dani rolled her eyes, playing with the remains of her omelette as she struggled with the knot that had formed in her stomach and had refused to shift since the night before. Her best friend of eighteen years usually always knew just how to pull her out of a dark mood, but her night with Valerio had shattered all the careful control she had worked so hard to achieve over the past few months. She felt completely off balance.

Hermione was no stranger to difficult situations, being the child of an infamous Los Angeles talent agent who had stolen money from half of Hollywood. They'd met as teenagers, on their first day at boarding school in England, when Hermione had stepped in to defend Dani from a group of name-calling older girls. Together they'd become untouchable, unrepentant overachievers all the way through college, supporting one another through the loss of parents, bad relationships and sanity.

Now that Hermione was one of the most in-demand personal stylists in Europe, they didn't get to see one another very often, but their emails were long and never short on salacious details.

Hermione called over a waiter and ordered a caramel-drizzled waffle from the extravagant dessert menu, declaring it a celebration after hearing Dani's heavily edited version of the events of the night before.

Dani shook her head. 'You're completely overlooking the part where he just assumed he could announce our engagement. Along with the rest of his little speech about keeping me safe by *marrying* me. I mean…who even *thinks* like that? Apparently "safe" is just another word for "away from my own sources of power and independence".'

'I don't know… Daniela Marchesi has got a nice ring to it.' Hermione smirked.

'You're taking far too much enjoyment from my outrage.'

'Sorry—a drop-dead gorgeous Italian, whom you used to have a gigantic crush on, is now back to run his own company, which might allow *you* to finally get back on track with starting your own PR firm.' She took a sip of her tea, her tone dry. 'Oh, and he apparently wants to marry you too. How utterly *terrible* all this is.'

Dani looked away from her friend, ignoring the tension in her body as she remembered that her own consulting work had come to a standstill since she'd taken the helm at Velamar. No one knew that she had signed a lease on an office in London just weeks before the awful news from Rio—that she'd finally been poised to quit her job at Velamar and launch her own firm.

But, truthfully, it had been easier to cancel all her plans and throw herself into the heavy workload that had come with being a stand-in CEO. There was less time to think, less time to feel...

Hermione continued to chatter, trying to lighten the mood in her usual way. 'With those eyes and that insane body... I wouldn't turn down *any* kind of dark and brooding proposal from Valerio Marchesi—that's all I'm saying.'

'I'm sorry that I don't share your love of dramatic romance. And I get it that he's a little paranoid since...since everything that happened in Rio. But I'm not in danger. This isn't Regency England and I am not on the market for a protector.'

She frowned as her phone buzzed with an email notification from the head of the Velamar events team.

Subject: You might be interested in this.

The email showed the guest list for the modest cocktail party she had planned for some select guests to get a sneak preview of the *Sirinetta II* later that evening. Dani frowned, her eyes scanning down the list with increasing disbelief.

A shocked huff of laughter escaped her lips. It seemed that Mr Hotshot CEO had decided to dive right back into work.

The numbers for the 'small and intimate' gathering had now tripled, and contained the names of some of the wealthiest people in Monaco, including philanthropists, celebrities and even a few members of European royalty. It was no secret that the Marchesi family had connections, but seriously...

The arrogance of the man! For him to just march over and amend details of an event that *she* had planned and executed without even asking...

The curse words that escaped her lips were very unladylike, sending even wild-mannered Hermione's eyebrows upwards.

'He believes he can just reappear and completely railroad an event that I've been planning for weeks! I bet he doesn't even think he's done anything wrong.'

She stabbed her index finger at the phone screen, beginning to type an email to inform her team that she didn't need to see the guest list, as she wouldn't be attending. Let the returned 'Playboy Pirate' explain her absence to his guests—let him try to make the same kind of connections and collaborations that she did at such events. He thought he could just swoop in and do everything? She would leave him to it.

Hermione interrupted her thoughts, bending to look at the email over her shoulder and letting out a low whistle. 'That's a lot of prime potential new clientele. What are you going to wear?'

'I won't go.' Dani bit her bottom lip. 'If he refuses to treat me like an equal partner in this company, then I don't see why I should jump to host this event by his side.'

'Correction, you *will* go. Because you *are* an equal partner in the company and a professional one at that. You'll go and you will tell him exactly where he can stick his proposal. Along with giving him a clear outline of the kind of treatment you will be expecting from now on.' Hermione opened up her small tablet computer and began clicking rapidly. 'I've got the perfect dress I've been saving for you—you just need to get the perfect date. And before you ask, I already have plans tonight.'

Dani knew her friend was right. The problem was that Valerio would also know that she couldn't *not* attend, and that grated on her nerves. 'If I do go, I won't need a date. I was the one to plan the thing originally, so I'm technically the hostess.'

Hermione had a familiar glimmer of mischief

in her eyes. 'You don't *need* one...but imagine what kind of statement it would make for you to walk into that party with the one man that Valerio Marchesi truly despises by your side.'

'You don't mean...?' Dani felt her eyes widen as she let out a puff of shocked laughter. 'I couldn't bring *him*. It would cause a riot. Besides, it's pretty late notice...'

'You think Tristan Falco isn't going to jump at the chance to gatecrash that party?'

Dani frowned, knowing her friend was right.

'You want to put Marchesi in his place, don't you?' Hermione waggled her brows. 'Time for you to introduce the ace up your sleeve. Show him that you're not playing nice. You make the call—I'll go and assemble my wonder team. That man has no idea who he's messing with.'

Hermione dropped a quick kiss on her cheek and breezed away, leaving Dani staring down at her phone, which was still open on the guest list.

She walked to the railing of the restaurant's terrace, looking out at the pink and orange clouds painted along the sky... The sun would start setting soon—she didn't have the luxury of waiting around. If she was going to put up a fight, she had to go to this event. Tomorrow she would come up with a new angle and figure out how to save Nettuno from being sold off. As for tonight...

She opened her phone and scrolled down to the name of a man she had never thought she would call again. A smile touched the corner of her lips as the number rang and a deep male voice answered. Within moments she had confirmed her scandalous date for the evening, silently marvelling at Hermione's evil genius.

It seemed that Cinderella *would* attend the ball after all, but she would not be waving the proverbial white flag and dancing with Prince Charming.

Tonight she would make Valerio Marchesi realise just how wrong he had been to underestimate her.

The paparazzi were gathered eagerly around the gates of Valerio's luxurious Monte Carlo villa, waiting for the first public photograph of the Playboy Pirate's return and an exclusive opportunity to see what had become of their tragic hero.

Valerio had planned to give them their show—to depart in his usual extravagant style, driving one of his prized sports cars. But at the last moment he had chosen to have his bodyguard drive one of the Jeeps, instructing him to exit the rear gate so that he could slip past the cameras.

He had told himself that he was adding to the

mystery—that he was playing up to the media circus and fanning the flames of gossip. It was all good publicity, after all. He was building up to a grand return on his own terms. But the reality was that he had stopped himself from booking the first flight out of Monaco at least three times since walking off the yacht into the dawn light that morning. If it hadn't been for the threat to Dani, he'd have gone. But he knew he had to be here—knew he had to ensure her complete safety.

He had stood in the marina, looking up at the now unfamiliar city that had once been one of his many playgrounds, and he had felt like an impostor. He was playing the part of Valerio Marchesi, but he had no interest in that life any more.

It all seemed so hollow now, as he looked back at the way he had lived. He had gone from one extreme to the next, proving himself in daring sailing challenges, throwing the wildest parties and seducing the most beautiful women. Life had just been one big adventure after another, with nothing ever big enough to satiate his appetite for more. Until everything had suddenly become tasteless and the thought of sailing or seducing had seemed just a waste of energy better spent on his investigations.

His old life seemed like a distant memory—

like the life of a stranger. But if he was no longer that version of himself...he had no idea *who* he was...

When he arrived at the party, his first priority was to ensure that Velamar's private marina was securely locked down. The elite security team he had hired six months ago had been expertly trained by the best in the business and they knew exactly where they needed to be. He stepped onto the main entertaining deck of the massive yacht to see that some of the guests had already arrived. A small swing band had set up on a small platform, and the intrusive bouncing melody of the music provided a perfect background for a night that would likely be filled with uncomfortable conversations and questions about his time away.

For the first time in months he wished he could down a few drinks as he was approached by several acquaintances all at once. But he'd long ago learned that drinking only made him feel worse. He needed to be in control of his senses, of his mind.

The party filled out quickly, and soon enough the entire room was watching him, the curiosity in their gazes mixed with the familiar sympathy he'd come to expect in the days immediately after his rescue. Hushed conversations began, ensuring that anyone who was *not* aware of the events that had put the scars on Valerio Marchesi's face and the growling darkness in his eyes was soon informed.

He had never lacked confidence about his looks—he knew that even despite the minor scarring and his leg injury he was still attractive enough. Some women would probably find it thrilling, seeing such a dramatic reminder of his fight for survival. They would build it into the fantasy of him as a rugged adventurer, like in the stories the media had loved to spread. But having so many eyes on him was a stark reminder of everything he would never outrun.

He would always be the scarred hero to them—someone both to pity and admire. None of them knew the truth of what had happened. None of them had lived through it.

But now was not the time to show weakness—not when he had important work to do. Being born a Marchesi meant he had been introduced to instant fame and pressure even before he could walk. He had chosen a different path from the family business, but he still used the lessons he had learned from his father every day. *When you feel weak, walk tall and look them in the eye.* So he met each set of curious eyes without hesitation, ignoring any mention of his absence and filling each conversation with talk of the latest yacht they planned to launch.

'Ah, here comes Daniela.' One of the members of the Velamar board craned her neck to look past him. 'Good grief—is that Tristan Falco on her arm?'

Every set of eyes in the small group around him snapped towards the steps at the opposite end of the long entertaining deck.

She wouldn't... Surely she would have the sense not to...

After seeing a series of nervous furtive glances towards him, Valerio gritted his jaw and turned to see for himself.

CHAPTER THREE

TIME SEEMED TO come to a standstill as his eyes
sought Dani across the crowd. She was shaking
hands with one of the politicians he'd invited,
the wide smile on her ruby-red lips a world away
from the indignant anger he'd last seen on her
face.

He was powerless to look away, and the tightness inside his chest loosened as he watched her
tilt her head back and laugh. She didn't even
have to try to be the perfect hostess—it just
came naturally.

As he looked on, the crowd tightened and
gathered around her, vying for her attention.
And even if he hadn't already been treading a
fine line with his control, seeing Tristan Falco
by her side had him fighting the insane urge
to growl.

There wasn't a single person on this yacht
who didn't know of his long-standing rivalry
with the heir to the Falco diamond fortune. He

shook his head, biting his lower lip to stop himself from laughing at such a deliberate power-play. Clever, infuriating woman. For some reason she was trying to provoke him…

As though she'd heard him, the object of his thoughts met his gaze across the sea of guests. Almost in slow motion, she raised her champagne glass in a toast, an unmistakable smirk on her full lips.

Schooling his own expression to one of mild interest, he raised his own in response and began to move slowly across the deck towards her. He could see her eyes shifting towards him at regular intervals as he got closer, her hand moving first to push an errant curl behind her ear, then to touch the delicate necklace at her throat.

He noticed that she had trapped her ebony curls high on her head, only letting a few hang free. It was impossible not to see how the style accentuated the long, bare expanse of her neck and shoulders, but likely that had been her aim. She was a confident woman—surely she knew how her appearance captivated the crowd around her.

He didn't know much about fashion, but he knew that she had chosen perfectly in the emerald-green concoction encasing her curves. He felt his throat turn dry as the shimmering material moved, revealing a modest slit up to the smooth skin of one thigh. Reflexively, he forced his gaze back to her face. She seemed to sparkle in the light as she moved away from the small crowd around her, taking a few steps in his direction to close the final gap between them.

'My compliments on your stellar work today, Mr CEO,' she said tightly, her charming smile still firmly in place as she waved politely at a couple of guests who passed them.

'I assumed you wouldn't mind my input on this event's inadequate guest list, seeing as you were so eager to have me back.' He fought the urge to smirk as her eyes sparked fire at him.

She took a delicate sip of her champagne, giving him an icy glare over the rim. 'If you had given me your input *before* making your sweeping changes, you might have found out that there was a strategic, brand-specific reason for my tiny guest list.'

'If you'd answered any of my calls today, maybe I could have done that.'

'Well, maybe I was too busy recovering from your ridiculous...*proposal*.' She lowered her voice to a hiss, her eyes darting around as she uttered the last word as though it were some kind of demonic chant.

Valerio couldn't help it then—he chuckled under his breath. There was absolutely nothing funny about any part of their situation, but some long-buried part of him was really enjoying this verbal sparring.

It had always been like this between them— from the first time they'd met as teenagers, when she'd come to watch Duarte in a sailing competition at their all-boys boarding school. Even when she'd joined Velamar he'd used to start fights with her at events just to draw out this...*fire*. At one point he'd started to wonder if she was avoiding him, and that had only made him try harder to provoke her—before Duarte had mistaken his playful jabs at her as interest and moved the entire PR and marketing division to their London offices. He'd said it wasn't because of that, but Valerio had known better.

The terse silence between them was broken by the arrival of a wide-smiling Tristan Falco at Dani's elbow. 'Marchesi, you seem to have forgotten my invitation tonight. Luckily your partner was in need of a fine male escort.'

'I wasn't aware that you were in town.' Valerio extended his hand to the other man, not missing the way Dani's eyes widened with surprise. 'I've never had the chance to thank you since the last time we spoke.'

A serious look came across the other man's features. 'It was nothing. I hope you took my advice.'

Valerio exhaled on a sigh, reflexively crossing his arms over his chest as he nodded brusquely. 'I did.'

'Am I missing something here?'

Dani's voice was hard as stone between them. Her hand was on her hip, her eyes narrowed as she looked from one man to the other. Tristan was the first to speak, sliding his arm over her shoulders and pulling her in close.

'It's a private matter between us guys.' He smiled in his trademark way. 'I met up with Marchesi a couple months back while I was in Rio.'

'Rio?' Dani fired that amber gaze Valerio's way briefly, then turned back and fluttered her lashes up at Tristan. 'How lovely. What did you guys get up to in lovely Rio?'

Valerio tensed, hoping Falco would have the good sense to stop talking. Despite his invaluable help, the man was still a thorn in his side. Even looking at him now, with his big meaty arm slung over Dani's shoulders, it made him want to throw a punch in his pretty-boy face and launch him bodily off the yacht.

After a long, painful silence it seemed Dani had realised that neither of them planned to elaborate further on the matter. But she didn't fire off another smart retort. Instead Valerio watched as a brief glimmer of hurt flashed in her eyes. Her lips thinned for a moment and she made a big display of looking around the party. Then she smiled—a glorious movement of red-painted lips and perfect teeth that seemed to hit him squarely in the chest.

'Excuse me, gentlemen... Some of us have work to do tonight.'

Valerio was powerless to do anything but watch as she retreated in the direction of the bar, stopping here and there to greet her guests cheerfully, as though nothing had happened at all. He cleared his throat, turning back to see Falco pointedly raising one eyebrow.

'Why do I feel like I'm interrupting something?' the other man drawled.

'Just a professional disagreement.' Valerio cleared his throat and took a long sip from his glass. 'None of your concern. Also, she's off-limits to you.'

'Professional?' Tristan Falco laughed. 'Right...and that's why you looked like you wanted to throw me overboard when you saw her with me.'

'There's still time if you don't stop talking,' Valerio said, gritting his teeth.

Falco raised both hands in mock surrender, leaning back against the wall to survey the crowd in his usual calculated way.

Valerio tried to ignore the pang of guilt in

his gut. He hadn't wanted Dani to find out that he'd been back to Brazil at all. And he certainly hadn't wanted her to find out like that.

She didn't know anything of the past six months of his life because he'd been trying to protect her from the worry that would come with the knowledge that he was still actively pursuing the men who had taken him and Duarte in Rio. That he had been knee-deep in a dangerous criminal underworld of corrupt politics and blackmail as he tried to piece together the events that had led to his best friend's death.

It had been pure chance that Tristan Falco had been in Rio at the same time. He'd saved Valerio from being arrested, drunk and ranting, after another lead had turned out to be useless.

The other man had cleaned him up and offered him some solid advice. *No more booze. Hire professionals to do the digging.* He'd also put Valerio in contact with a discreet and highly qualified clinician to help with the psychological aspects of his recovery. And he'd shared some of his contacts to help Valerio dig into the backgrounds of some of the men he suspected of involvement. The diamond heir had become an unlikely ally in his fight for justice.

Valerio took the first opportunity to move away in search of his unhappy business partner. He had made his peace with Falco, but that didn't mean he was suddenly able to tolerate his company for longer than necessary.

He moved through the crowd, hating how uneasy and wooden he felt when he stopped to converse with his guests. His smile felt too tight, his shoulders heavy. The old Valerio would have been in his element here, not counting down the minutes until it would be acceptable for him to slip away.

This conflict with Daniela had got under his skin. Clearly she was annoyed by his actions today—which, honestly, he'd expected. He hadn't planned to triple her guest list, but it added to his mission to draw attention to his social standing and good connections. An unstable CEO would hardly host a party for all of Monaco's elite, would he? Plus, he'd been frustrated at her reaction to his proposal. He felt an urgency to his plans now and he needed her to stop fighting him.

The trouble was, he didn't want to reveal the full truth of her situation and scare her away. He had planned to find a balance tonight, to give her just enough incentive to co-operate and accept his proposal. She was no fainting little miss, that was for sure—especially considering she had quite literally kidnapped him to ensure she got him to Monte Carlo.

But his plans for tonight had not involved

having her completely furious with him. He needed her by his side. It was the only way he could keep her safe.

Discomfort had him running a finger along the rim of his collar, fighting the urge to rip off his tie and open a few buttons. He had chosen the open decks of the yacht deliberately, knowing that confined spaces were one of his triggers. But it seemed that even having the entire night sky above him was not enough to stop the familiar tingle of hyper-awareness from creeping up his spine. Every loud bark of laughter and clink of glassware brought a shot of tension painful enough to have him gritting his teeth.

A movement on the opposite side of the sea terrace caught his eye. One of Daniela's security men, conferring with the rest of the team with a worried look on his face. Valerio moved forward, the tension mounting in his gut like a furnace.

One brief exchange of words with the men was enough to confirm his worst fear.

She was missing.

Dani had moved away from the crowd initially just needing a moment to herself. That moment had turned into a quarter of an hour as she'd wandered through the yacht in search of privacy. Finally she'd emerged onto an open seaview terrace at the stern, breathing a sigh of relief to find it empty but cursing herself for not grabbing another glass of champagne or some canapés. She hadn't eaten a lot after her brunch with Hermione, and already she could feel the buzz of alcohol in her head. She'd always been a lightweight.

From their current position, she could see the lights of Monte Carlo twinkling like fiery diamonds above the water. She could see the glow of the iconic Monaco Naval Museum and the Grimaldi Forum in the distance. Such beauty would usually bring her a sense of calm, but nothing seemed able to rid her of the restless feeling that had plagued her all day.

Her late entrance to the party had been calculated to ensure the maximum effect of the majestic, glittering emerald gown Hermione had provided. Its designer was a new hot name on the Paris runway, his trademark exclusive material a blissfully comfortable stretch velvet that had actual diamond fragments threaded throughout.

The piece was heaven for the more curvaceous women of the world, like her. It moulded to her body like a second skin and flared out slightly just below her knees in a delicate flounce. And the *pièce de résistance* to complement her perfect ensemble was the man she'd had on her arm.

What on earth had she been thinking, bringing Tristan Falco? Everyone else on the yacht had watched that ridiculous display of thoroughly masculine camaraderie between him and Valerio with a mixture of appreciation and curiosity. She had heard whispers—one person wondering if this finally meant a partnership of the two brands was in the works...another dreamily wishing that *she* could be in the middle of the two hunks.

Dani didn't know what bothered her more: all those women drooling over the two men or the fact that most of the guests would attribute any future partnership between Falco Diamonds and Velamar to Valerio's presumed genius.

Dani had been approached by Tristan numerous times in the past few months about a possible collaboration between their two brands. It was no secret that Valerio had firmly declined his numerous offers in the past, even though it made perfect business sense for the two to join forces, considering the strong history already present between Falco Diamonds and the other members of the wealthy Marchesi family.

The soft clearing of a throat brought her back to the moment. She turned, expecting to see that Valerio had followed her, but instead she was met with the sight of a thin man with a shock of salt-and-pepper hair that seemed vaguely familiar. There was a kind of meanness in the smile he gave her, and a shrewdness in the way he scanned the empty deck area with a seeming lack of interest.

'*Boa noite*, Senhorita Avelar.'

His voice was reedy, as though he smoked twenty cigarettes a day. A few steps closer and the odour that drifted off his expensive suit confirmed her theory. She held her breath as the man leaned forward to place the customary kiss on her right cheek.

'Angelus Fiero—I'm an old friend of your father's and a silent member of the board.' He smiled, extending a flute of champagne towards her. 'I hope you don't mind me following you?'

She accepted the glass, pasting a polite smile on her face and ignoring the shiver of unease in her spine. He took a seat directly across from her on a low cushioned bench that bordered the delicate curved rail of the deck.

'You seem to be taking your job as CEO very seriously. I have heard of your divine talent. Ruling with an iron fist and a perfect smile. Turning things from rotten wood into finely polished oak,' he said cryptically, with a strange glimmer in his eyes. 'Tell me…is it a new company protocol to bypass a direct order from the executor of someone's will?'

Dani paused, the champagne flute inches from her lips.

'I'd bet Marchesi has no idea that *you* were the one to apply for Duarte's death certificate, has he?'

Dani initially fought the urge to shout that Valerio was not her keeper. But then her logical brain processed the man's words and she didn't speak, her mind utterly frozen in confusion. Who *was* this man, with his all too knowing eyes and his knowledge of top-secret information?

There was no proof that she'd been the one to file the request for Duarte's death certificate—she'd used a notary and the company name as a group entity. Not that she'd been planning to keep it a secret—not until Valerio's furious reaction, anyway. She'd planned to tell him eventually.

She couldn't really explain her urge to have the limbo of her brother's death put into legal black and white. It had been an intolerable hum of sadness and a slow bubble of frustration—like an itch under her skin that she couldn't scratch. She'd known she couldn't wait around for Valerio to return and decide to accept that Duarte's death was a reality.

But now, on this dark, secluded part of the yacht, a part of her became suddenly painfully aware of the fact that she had put herself in a vulnerable position, out here alone without any of her security team.

Fiero stood up, taking a few steps to close the gap between them. Dani fought the urge to stand and run, taking note of his distance from her and feeling the weight of the empty champagne glass in her hands. She was alone, but she was not incapable of self-defence. She straightened her shoulders, meeting his gaze with what she hoped was a perfectly calm expression.

'I came here tonight to give you a warning. If you value your life, stop digging into things that don't concern you.'

Dani inhaled sharply at the threat, watching as the older man turned to walk away.

His route was suddenly barred by the arrival of three security guards in the doorway and a thunder-faced Valerio, who took one look at Daniela's ashen face and immediately cornered their guest.

'Marchesi.' Fiero spoke calmly, placing a cigarette between his lips and lighting it. 'Nice to see you again. Is there some sort of problem?'

'I don't know yet.' Valerio looked the man up and down, his fists clenched at his sides. 'Daniela?'

Valerio said her name softly, but with a stern undertone that had her snapping out of the daze she was in. 'Everything is fine,' she heard herself say. 'Let him go.'

She was vaguely aware of Valerio ordering the security men to escort Fiero back to the party and keep a close eye on the man. He waited until they were alone on the deck, then took a few steps towards her, crossing his arms in that way he did when he was intensely annoyed by something.

It amazed her that she could still tell his mood just by observing his body language, considering how little they had seen one another in the past few years. She was lucky he couldn't do the same with her, or he'd know just how absolutely terrified she felt. A shiver ran down her spine as she looked up at the thunderous expression on his face.

'Disappearing alone without protection— have you lost your mind?'

'We're on a yacht.' She rolled her eyes. 'Also, I'm a grown woman, Valerio. Not a child for you to keep track of and scold.'

'Even a child would know not to risk its own safety by wandering off alone into the darkness.'

He blocked her path when she tried to move away, placing one hand on her arm.

'Why did you come out here, Dani? What could Angelus Fiero possibly have to say to you?'

Her mind kept replaying those words over and over on a loop.

'If you value your life.'

'If you value your life.'

She felt the heat of Valerio's hand on her arm, sinking into her skin like a brand. She tried to draw on her anger at him for disappearing, for leaving her to run Velamar alone while she tried to hide her own grief. She shouldn't feel this urge to fall into the safety of him when he had done nothing but give orders and trample on her work in all his six-foot-four and ridiculously handsome glory.

He had kept his newfound peace with Tristan Falco from her, and his apparent trip to Rio, and God only knew what else. He made her utterly furious.

She tried to remember all the reasons she might throw at him for why she had walked out…other than the fact that she'd needed to get away from him and the way he made her feel completely off balance. But now, with his simple touch burning against her arm, she was powerless even to control the erratic beating of her own stupid heart.

He frowned down at his hand on her arm,

dropping it away as though he hadn't realised he was touching her.

'He was just expressing his condolences in person for our loss. He couldn't come to the memorial service.' Dani felt the lies fall easily from her lips, guilt pressing at her conscience as she turned and began walking back through the yacht towards the faint strains of the string quartet and the sound of laughter.

'Stop running from me. I need to speak with you alone.' He easily moved around her in the darkened study and blocked her way. 'You arrived here tonight with that womanising fool on your arm without any thought other than angering me.'

'Why would I care what you think, Valerio? You clearly don't do the same for me.'

'You don't see a slight problem with bringing a date to your *fiancé's* event?'

Dani froze in disbelief, the word 'fiancé' coming from his lips sending her blood pressure into overdrive. The man had lost his mind entirely.

'Again this ridiculous promise you made? Valerio... I've already made it quite clear what I think about your proposal. It's completely unnecessary.'

She took a step backwards, needing to put physical space between them. No one made her quite as angry as he did. No one else could manage to get under her skin and surpass her control.

'I'm not some damsel in distress who needs your protection. Until this morning I was acting CEO of the company we share equal ownership of. I've been at the helm of Velamar for six months while I gave you the time you needed to recover.'

'I don't think you're a damsel in distress. You are the strongest woman I've ever met. I just need you to trust me that we need to do this.'

'It doesn't make sense. I wouldn't let Duarte make this choice for me if he were alive. And I won't be accepting it from you, either.'

'This isn't about how capable you are. This is about your safety.'

Suddenly her anger fell away and she looked at him. Took in the tension around his mouth, the shadows in his eyes. She remembered his reaction when she'd told him that Duarte was soon to be declared legally dead. She had seen something entirely different then. He hadn't just been angry... He'd been afraid. For *her*. And then her mind replayed the look on his face as he'd arrived just now with the three guards in tow, asking her if there was a problem.

'Look... I haven't been truthful about what I've been doing for the past six months. You thought I was in hiding while I recovered and I let you believe that because it's partially true. I have been isolated and angry and dealing with… with what happened. Tristan Falco witnessed my own methods of dealing with it first-hand and gave me some good advice.'

'No more lies and avoidance. Tell me the truth. Why do you need me to agree to this so badly?' As she asked the question, her legs felt weak, and an odd twisting sensation started up in her stomach.

He smoothed a hand down his face, closing his eyes for a long moment as though fortifying himself.

'Duarte knew that he was in danger when he went to Rio alone. He didn't expect me to follow him. All I know is that he was being blackmailed. I couldn't get a full picture of who was behind it or what had gone down before I arrived and everything went to hell, but I do know that he was trying to neutralise an imminent threat…to you both.'

Dani felt the breath completely leave her chest as she sat down on a nearby chair, looking up at him with disbelief. 'If I'm in danger… If they've already got Duarte…'

'Daniela, look at me.' He knelt down, gripping her chin between his fingers and forcing her to meet his eyes. 'I won't let anyone hurt you. I've spent months trying to find another way to help because I knew you would hate this. The only thing I'm sure of is that it has to do with part of your inheritance. The land and properties in Brazil.'

'They can have it—I never wanted any of it.' She breathed in, feeling her pulse careening out of control. This was insanity—utter madness. She'd give everything away…every single cent. Nothing was worth the loss she'd endured. *Nothing.*

'I thought of that.' Valerio spoke softly, as though he feared he had fully tipped her over the edge. 'But it's complicated. We're talking about decades of your parents' work in creating affordable housing there. Tens of thousands of innocent tenants who stand to be displaced. Acres of protected land being put at risk.'

Tens of thousands… Dani closed her eyes and felt a tremor within her.

Her father had been an only child, sole heir to the wealthiest, most corrupt landowner in Brazil. When his old man had died, her *papai* had been newly married to his very liberal-minded English wife. Together they had wasted no time in setting out on a crusade to turn the majority of their expensive, undeveloped inner-city land into rent-controlled housing initiatives for disadvantaged families. It had been revolutionary, and it had angered a lot of wealthy developers by the time they'd started on the city of Rio.

'Dani...' Valerio said. 'As a married couple, we can create an iron-clad prenuptial agreement that ties all your assets to mine. We need to make them untouchable, so that there's no valid reason for anyone to target you. My family name, the legal power it holds... It's like a fortress. Duarte knew that. He'd planned for it if his efforts didn't succeed.'

Dani shuddered, the reality of her situation settling like a frost on her skin. She and her brother had been targeted for something they had no control over. She had never asked to be born into this life... She hadn't asked for her entire family to be taken away from her in a matter of years.

She felt her throat contract painfully as she tried to force breath in and out.

'Do you understand now why it needs to be this way?' he said softly, coming round to look into her eyes. 'I need you to stop fighting me on this. I need you to put your trust in me and let me keep you safe.'

She couldn't meet his eyes. This was all far too much to handle without the effect he had on her added to the mix too.

She simply nodded once. 'I'll do it.'

'I'm sorry I couldn't find another way.'

She tried not to wince at his words. Tried not to imagine his horror when he'd realised he was going to have to shackle himself in matrimony to a woman he could barely tolerate. A woman he seemed to actively avoid even though they'd been working for the same company for years.

'You don't need to pretend that this is what you want. It is what it is, Valerio.' She stood up, smoothing down her dress in an effort to compose herself even as her voice shook. 'We need to get back to the party or they'll start talking about us… Although I suppose I'm going to have to get used to that if I'm about to marry you.'

Something glittered in his eyes as she said those words. Whether it was relief or dread, she didn't take the time to find out. She needed to get away from the strange intimacy of being here in the darkness with him. Back to the safety of the party, to networking, putting on a show.

'You will have to get used to a lot of things.' His gaze drifted away, his jaw tightening. 'We both will.'

Dani smiled tightly, turning and walking along the corridor, then up the stairs to the entertaining deck. She heard him following silently behind her, but didn't pause until they were safely on the sidelines of the dance floor, where the music made it slightly harder to hear him without leaning in.

'I'm making our announcement here…tonight.'

His voice travelled slowly across the din of music and voices, and Dani frowned, his meaning taking a moment to sink in. Her eyes widened as he moved to step away, and her fingers clutched at the sleeve of his jacket to stop him.

'If you're talking about what I think you are…'

He moved close, dipping his head to speak close to her ear. 'We are on a superyacht, filled with the most famous people in Europe. If we want news of our engagement to travel fast, then there's no time like the present.'

Dani shook her head, hardly believing what a turn the evening had taken. 'Okay…but there's no need for it to be a big deal. It doesn't have to be a spectacle.'

'You know it does.'

He smiled, and for a moment she got a glimpse of his old self. Mischievous and eager to cause a stir.

'I'm going to make sure the whole world knows you are about to become my wife.'

CHAPTER FOUR

'OH, GOD…' DANI breathed, staring up into the
azure blue depths of his eyes and praying that
she could maintain her composure. She looked
around at the beautiful people surrounding
them, oblivious to the fact that her entire world
had shifted on its axis. 'We can just make the
announcement tomorrow somewhere…please.'

'This needs to be convincing, Daniela.'

His voice was gravelly and low in her ear,
making her skin prickle. She knew he was right.
This was the kind of guest list, with the kind
of publicity reach, that could undo every single bit of questionable press Velamar had got in
the past six months. It was the perfect way to
take control of the media narrative while also
taking steps to secure her safety. She tried not
to imagine the backlash—the sniped remarks
about why a man like him would choose her.

She prided herself on being self-sufficient.
On having walked away from her ex because

he'd assumed that she would change her iron-clad life plan to fit around him. And now here she stood, contemplating entwining her life and everything she owned with the one person she had sworn never to trust again. This wild, reckless playboy had somehow become the only solid land within reach in a dangerous sea.

She shook her head, hardly believing what she was about to do. 'Okay, but…but you need to get down on one knee,' she breathed, hardly believing the words coming out of her mouth.

'Are you organising my proposal?' His eyes sparkled with mirth. 'Do you have a preference for which knee I use?'

'Be serious. Just… It's more romantic that way.'

One dark brow rose in disbelief, and for a moment she expected him to argue. But then he raised both hands in mock surrender and took a step backwards.

A single gesture to a nearby server gave a signal that he wished to grab everyone's attention. Somewhere nearby silverware was clinked gently against a glass and a lull fell over the party, the string quartet slowing their melody to a stop. Dani felt her heartbeat pound in her ears as Valerio met her eyes and then lowered his impressive frame gracefully down onto one knee.

Dani tried not to be hyper-aware of the dozens and dozens of stunned eyes and gasped breaths as everyone became glued to the tableau unfolding in their midst. It was one thing to be in business mode amongst them, but this was so far out of her comfort zone she almost felt like taking her chances overboard. Never mind her lifelong terror of swimming in the open sea—anything was preferable to feeling this exposed.

Valerio looked up at her, and for a moment, Dani forgot to breathe. This painfully gorgeous man was every woman's dream. It was almost too much to take in the sincerity on his handsome features as he cleared his throat and reached for her hand. And she had never understood the term *fluttering* when it came to heartbeats, but there was no other way to describe the strange thrumming in her chest as Valerio gently lowered his lips and pressed a featherlight kiss against her fingers.

'This will come as a shock to many of you, but Daniela and I have been keeping a large part of our life private for a long time now.' Valerio's voice sounded huskier, his accent more pronounced, and his eyes never wavered from hers as he continued. 'Darling, I know we said we would wait, but I want to share this moment with our guests. Daniela Avelar, will you do me the honour of becoming my wife?'

Dani was painfully aware of the silence around them. She nodded, her chin bobbing up and down like a puppet on a string, forcing a wide smile and praying that she didn't look as terrified as she felt. Applause began to resound around them as their guests cheered and fawned over them.

She swallowed hard, her eyes widening as she noticed the small velvet box he had produced from his coat pocket. The ring inside was an antique canary-yellow diamond that she knew instantly would match the gold heirloom wedding band she had inherited from her mother.

She tensed at the realisation that he had come so prepared for this moment. Had he been so sure that she would agree to this madness? Suddenly, the huge guest list made even more sense.

Her hand shook against Valerio's warm skin as he slid the ring onto her third finger. It was a perfect fit.

He stood, his eyes darkening with some strange emotion as he pulled her against his hard chest and buried his face next to her ear. 'I'm going to kiss you now, Daniela. Try to pretend you're enjoying it.'

His arm tightened around her waist as his lips easily found hers. The kiss was initially just a gentle press of skin against skin. Dani tried to remain impartial to the searing heat of the large male hand on her hip and at the nape of her neck, but she shivered reflexively at the contact. He was so... *large* all around her... he somehow made her feel small.

She was being ridiculous. She needed to keep a level head here. But when the delicious scent of his cologne enveloped her, she couldn't help her own reflexive movement and she traced her tongue along the seam of his lips. It had been so long since she'd been kissed that her body seemed to jolt with electricity as a mortifying groan emanated from deep in her throat.

Valerio seemed to stiffen at the noise, and for a moment she fully expected him to move away. He would know that she wasn't just pretending. But instead he pulled her even tighter against his body, deepening the kiss and giving back just as good as he got. His movements were much more skilful than her own shy ones, and his lips and tongue moved slowly against hers in such a perfectly seductive rhythm she quickly lost the ability to think straight.

She had never been kissed this way. It was as if she'd spent her life believing she knew all there was to know about her own body and now he was just tearing everything down.

Her mind screamed at her to slow down, to stop falling for this act they were putting on, but her body flat-out refused to listen. Already she could feel herself become embarrassingly aroused, heat spreading through her like wildfire. She reached up and spread her fingers through his hair, down to the warmth of his nape under the collar of his shirt, needing to feel more of him under her fingertips.

When her nail accidentally scraped his skin, the groan that came from deep in his throat shocked her to her core. It was quite possibly the most erotic sound that she had ever heard in her life.

Of course he would choose that exact moment to rip himself away from her. His eyes were wide with a mixture of shock and anger, and he watched her for a long moment, both of them breathing heavily as they became aware of their surroundings once more.

Dani fought the urge to pull him straight back, then felt her cheeks heat with embarrassment at how quickly she'd lost control. The whole thing had probably lasted no more than a minute and yet she felt as though time had ceased to exist.

The swing band resumed their music with a loud, jazzy celebratory number, and the guests began gathering inward, everyone bustling over to give them their good wishes. Flutes of champagne were handed out and soon they were swept away on an endless stream of toasts and congratulations.

And all the while Dani was painfully aware of the man by her side, of every small touch of his hand at her back or dip of his head to speak close to her ear.

She thanked the heavens when he finally moved away to another group of people, feeling as if she was pulling air into her lungs after being underwater. It had been far too long since she'd had any contact with a member of the opposite sex, she thought. She felt as though every nerve-ending in her body had been lit up like a firework. And now the mad urge to seek him out in the crowd every few minutes plagued her consciousness. She couldn't concentrate, couldn't relax with these knots in her stomach.

A few glasses of champagne later and she was significantly less wound up, but the exhaustion of the past twenty-four hours was crashing down on her like a freight train.

The more distinguished guests disappeared once they'd docked back at the marina, leaving a younger, energetic crowd, who seemed to be only just getting started on their evening of partying.

Just as she began to wonder if anyone would notice if she slipped away to bed, she felt two warm hands slide around her waist from behind.

'I think it's time for me to take my fiancée home,' Valerio said, addressing the small gathering of remaining guests over her shoulder.

'No, I can go alone. You should stay—' She turned towards him, gently removing his hands from their possessive grip on her hips.

He simply tightened his hold, a low chuckle coming from deep in his throat as he leaned down, his lips so close to her ear it sent another eruption of shivers down her spine.

'That's not how a newly engaged couple should behave. At least try to act like you can't wait to get me to bed,' he said quietly, and then he raised his voice to address their remaining guests. 'I believe Falco mentioned wanting to host an after-party back at his place—isn't that right?'

Tristan Falco, who had been sitting with a beautiful blonde actress, stood up, a teasing smile on his lips. 'Considering I've just put in an order for one of these wonderful vessels, I think I'll stay on board tonight—if that's all right with you?'

'Stay as long as you need.' Dani smiled. 'If you have any problems, I'll be sleeping just down—'

'She'll be unavailable because we're going home.' Valerio cut across her, one hand caressing her shoulder as he spoke. 'Please take your time and enjoy the rest of your night.'

With barely a moment to protest, Dani felt herself deftly manoeuvred away from the group and across the empty entertainment deck.

'Valerio, I'm not going home with you. For goodness' sake...all my things are here,' she finished weakly, a mixture of champagne bubbles and exhaustion weighing heavily on her brain's ability to function.

'I've already had them moved to my villa.'

She paused at the edge of the dance floor, narrowing her eyes up at him. 'I get it that I should be grateful that you're helping me. But the next time you decide to organise something that involves my active participation and *my* personal things, I'd appreciate if you clear it with me first.'

'Dani...'

He began to protest, but she'd suddenly had enough of talking for the night. She stepped around him, moving down the lamplit ramp and into the dark confines of his chauffeur-driven car before he could see how completely unravelled she'd become.

If silence was a weapon, Daniela Avelar wielded it with damning precision. Valerio had spent the entire drive from the marina to his coastal villa on edge as she faced away from him. He'd expected her outrage at his heavy-handed behaviour, but this passive silence was something he had never experienced from her. It was unnerving. They still had things to discuss about their arrangement.

Once they were safely inside the foyer, he steeled himself for a showdown—but his housekeeper appeared and offered to show her to her room. Dani practically ran up the stairs away from him before he could wish her goodnight.

He fought the urge to follow her, to force her to meet his eyes. To acknowledge him in some way. They were about to be married, for goodness' sake, and she was acting as if he was some kind of villain, trying to take away her freedom. Didn't she see that everything he'd done had been with *her* at the forefront of his consideration?

And then there was that kiss…

He shook his head. He wasn't going to think about the kiss. They'd both known it was just a part of the act they were putting on. It wasn't *her* fault that he'd responded as he had…like a starving man with his first taste of sustenance… He'd wanted to devour her.

His body responded to the memory so powerfully that he jumped when his phone began to ring and shook him from his erotic thoughts.

AMANDA CINELLI   85

Looking at the number on the screen, he steeled himself for more bad news.

The call from his private investigations team took less than five minutes and told him everything he'd already suspected. Someone on the board at Velamar had applied for Duarte's death certificate without any clearance from him.

He felt a sick twist of nausea in his gut at the realisation that someone close to Velamar was behind all this. He remembered the look in Angelus Fiero's eyes as he'd moved away from Daniela on that darkened deck earlier. How pale she'd looked. He needed to share this information with her...ask her if Fiero had mentioned anything suspicious.

He thanked his housekeeper as she locked up for the night, then shrugged off his jacket and folded it over a nearby chair before climbing the stairs. To his surprise, the door to the main guest room was slightly open, a glow of golden light shining out onto the darkened hallway. She was still up.

He paused outside. He needed to press her further about Fiero... He had a feeling that there was something she wasn't telling him. And it had nothing to do with wanting to ask her why she had kissed him back so passionately. Or the fact that the memory of the way her fingers had slid up through his hair refused to shift from his mind.

He knocked once on the door, opening it a little more, then froze as he took in the sight before him. Dani sat fully dressed on the chaise in the corner of the room, her tablet computer glowing on her lap but her head thrown back at an angle in peaceful sleep.

Guilt assailed him; she probably hadn't got much sleep with all the dramatics the night before. She must have been exhausted and yet she hadn't complained once.

She would ache in the morning if he left her in her current position... He took a few steps closer, clearing his throat in case he startled her. 'Dani...?'

She didn't move. She looked as utterly composed in sleep as she did when she was awake—no snores escaped her lips, and even her legs were tucked perfectly to one side.

He gently tapped her shoulder, repeating her name once more. She was completely out.

Making a snap decision, he set her computer aside and lifted her from the chaise, depositing her gently on top of the bed. Her eyes drifted open, her hands moving up to touch his face.

'You kissed me tonight...' she slurred softly, eyes half closed.

'I did,' he said stiffly, removing her hands

and pushing her down to the pillows so that he could pull up the bedcovers and leave.

'I usually hate kissing,' she mumbled. 'But you're really good at it.'

'You're not so bad yourself.'

'It's okay. I know I'm terrible. I'm awful at everything bedroom-related—it's a curse of some sort.' She made a sound halfway between a giggle and a hum.

Valerio froze, staring down at her as he processed her nonsensical words. 'What makes you think that?'

'My ex was very honest. Oh, wait—you're supposed to take off my dress.' She closed her eyes, raising her arms above her head. 'I can't sleep in it. Hermione will kill me.'

'I draw the line at undressing unconscious women, even to save a designer dress.'

He'd gritted his teeth at her mention of her ex, but now he sucked in a breath as her hands began pulling at the hem of the dress and moving it upwards. He averted his eyes, steeling himself against the flash of delicious caramel skin in the lamplight. A tiny squeaking sound caught his attention, and he looked back to find her trapped inside a swathe of green fabric, her hands fumbling over her head.

Of course she wore no bra.

Cursing, Valerio pushed her hands away, then

gently pulled the gown the rest of the way up over her shoulders and arms. The tension in his body mounted with the effort of trying not to notice the delicious curves revealed with every pull of the fabric. He averted his eyes as much as possible, fighting the flare of heat in his solar plexus at an unavoidable glimpse of a tiny pair of lacy red knickers.

Biting his bottom lip, he quickly covered her with the bedsheet and sat back, his breath coming fast, as if he'd just run a marathon. He was not any better for that three-second sight of her naked breasts. He imagined they would spill over his palms, perfect twin globes, with dusky tips just begging to be kissed. His heartbeat thundered in his ears, a fine sheen of sweat was forming on his brow, and his blood pressure was likely rising through the roof.

But then Dani sighed, and he couldn't stop himself from looking down at her as she stretched out like a cat in sunshine. He had never seen her so still. The woman was a force of nature—always on the move. He wondered when she'd last taken a vacation, or even a day off.

He eased back, planning to slip out, but she opened her eyes again, narrowing them on him.

'I want to kiss you again.' She reached for

him, her fingertips sloppily tracing the column of his throat where his shirt hung open.

'I can't tell if you're drunk from too much champagne or overtiredness.' He tried to ignore the rush of pleasure her words gave him, knowing that the sober Daniela would be mortified. 'I need to go.'

'Don't leave me.' She opened her eyes more fully, their whisky-gold depths suddenly shimmering. 'Just lie here for a little while.'

Valerio felt the air in his lungs go cold at the vulnerability in her eyes. He had only ever seen her cry once, in the entire time they had known one another.

He sat back down on the bed, taking her hand in his and pressing her fingers to his lips. 'I'll stay a moment if you promise to sleep.'

Her eyes drifted closed and she sighed, the evidence of her sadness trailing from the corner of her eyes and down her cheeks. 'Everyone always leaves…' she whispered, half asleep.

Valerio felt something deep inside him crack at the pain in her words and he reached down to wipe the moisture from her cheek. He closed his eyes, inhaling once before looking down at her sleeping form. 'I'm not going anywhere.'

He shed his shoes, wincing at the stiffness in his injured leg as he lay back on the bed alongside her sleeping form. His fiancée had revealed far more tonight than she would likely have preferred.

He thought of her words—'my ex was very honest'. His fists tightened by his sides and he resisted the urge to wake her and demand to know exactly what her idiotic English lawyer ex had said. He had never met the man, couldn't even recall his name, but he had heard enough from Duarte to know that Dani deserved more.

Still, the violence of his outrage on her behalf was enough to stop him in his tracks. But it was entirely appropriate for him to feel protective towards the woman he'd vowed to protect, wasn't it?

There had been nothing 'appropriate' about his reaction to their kiss earlier. Nothing innocent or protective in the way he'd fought the urge to haul her towards him and devour her. Claim her as his own in front of the entire party—including Tristan Falco.

But he knew that he was not the kind of man she deserved, either. She needed someone whole. Someone who didn't abandon her and keep secrets. He had always been happy to live the life of a bachelor, thinking that maybe one day he might settle down. But now he knew that day would never come.

He wasn't built for family life the way his father and brother were. The Marchesi men were known for their reliable leadership and levelheadedness. Somehow Valerio seemed to have missed out on that genetic component and that had always been fine with him. He was the wild one...the joker.

Cursing under his breath, he closed his eyes and saw again Daniela's golden gaze meeting his as he slid that ring onto her finger. For that split second she hadn't looked as if she hated him quite as much.

They both knew that even if it was only a legal arrangement this marriage needed to look real. Neither of them could afford any bad press, and the distraction of their supposed romance would work in their favour. He needed to make sure she understood what that meant. He needed to know she understood that while she might deserve better, for now he was the only man she would be seen with.

Forcing himself to look away from her sleeping form, he rested his head back against the pillows. He would stay until he was sure she was asleep—surely he owed her that much?

Not for the first time since he had woken up to see her furious form twenty-four hours before, he wondered how on earth his life had become so complicated.

Dani awoke with the most painful headache of her entire life, inwardly cursing whoever had thought endless flutes of champagne was a good idea—then realised that it had, in fact, been her. She rolled over in the bed, freezing, and realised she was wearing only her underwear. Not only that—she wasn't alone in bed.

Valerio lay on his back, one arm behind his head as he slept. Fuzzy memories of him helping her to bed came to her, making her flush with embarrassment. She had practically ordered him to take her clothes off and then begged him to stay. Good grief, had she really told him about the things Kitt had said to her?

She stared at his sleeping form for a long while, noting the deep frown line between his brows and the sharp staccato of his breathing. There was nothing peaceful about the way this man slept—it was as though he were in pain. Even as she watched, he kicked out one leg at some invisible form, and a deep rumble sounded from his chest.

She sat up, clutching the covers to her bare breasts, and laid one hand on his chest. His hand shot up to grab hers so fast she jumped with fright.

It seemed one moment she was staring at him, the next he was gripping her shoulders painfully tight and pushing her onto her back. He loomed over her, caging her with his arms, and for a moment she felt a flash of unease at the zoned-out look in his eyes.

She pushed at his chest, feeling the silk of his shirt and the heat of his hard muscles under her fingers. It was like trying to shift a hulking great pillar of marble. Had he always been this physically defined? She tried to find words, only managing a tiny gasp in the tense silence.

He watched her through hooded eyes, barely controlled violence in the tension of his shoulders. But when she let out a small whimper from the force of his grip, something finally seemed to shift in his eyes, as if he had only just awoken.

'*Dannazione*…never touch me while I sleep,' he rasped.

'You…you're the one in my bed.' She pursed her lips, all too aware of her lack of clothing and the intimacy of their position. The thin sheet was the only thing covering her body from his gaze.

Her mind went back two nights, to when he'd attacked her bodyguards on his yacht in Genoa. He had been awoken from sleep then too. His eyes had been wild and unfocused, as though he had been possessed.

'Did I hurt you?' he asked quietly, his eyes scanning the bare skin of her arms as though he expected to see something terrible there.

She watched as he swept his fingers up her arms, seeing the faint red skin on her shoulders from his grip. He tucked his fingers under her chin, gently tilting her face up to look at him.

'No, you were just startled. It's fine,' she said shakily. 'I'm fine.'

His head momentarily sagged against her, his forehead pressing gently on her collarbone as he let out a long, shaky breath.

'Do you see now? This is why I stayed away for so long. Every damn time I feel like I'm getting it all under control…'

She felt every breath he took fanning gently against her skin. It was shockingly intimate.

All too soon she felt him pull away. He sat up on the side of the bed, leaving her shivering at the sudden loss of his heat. She wanted to ask him what he was talking about, if these moments of trance-like behaviour happened often. But she feared him shutting down, freezing her out again. She needed to wait for him to open up, no matter how much she craved to know what had happened to him during those awful weeks and the months that followed.

She sat up, moving beside him and fighting the urge to cover one of his large hands with her own. She couldn't stop wanting to touch him, to be near him. It was ridiculous—she was supposed to hate the man.

'Look…you don't have to tell me any details. But you didn't hurt me, okay?'

He stood up, hissing briefly as he straightened his leg. Avoiding her eyes, he set about buttoning his shirt. 'Those marks on your shoulder say otherwise.' He looked back at her, cursing under his breath. 'Don't worry. I won't let it happen again.'

Dani frowned, realising that was the opposite of what she wanted. She had been surprised to wake up to find him in bed beside her, but it had been the kind of surprise that sent shivers down your spine, not fear. She had worried that he might be able to sense her response to having him there with her, but stopped now she saw the familiar look of detachment cover his handsome features.

She could understand him being angry, and possibly embarrassed by whatever she had witnessed, but the complete blankness that had descended over him made her grip the blanket tighter across her chest.

'You'll join me for breakfast on the terrace.' He avoided her eyes, and his words were more of a command than an invitation. 'I'll leave you to…get dressed.'

His movements were stilted, the injury in his leg more pronounced as he stalked over to the doorway and disappeared without another word.

CHAPTER FIVE

WHEN DANI EMERGED from her room, she was freshly showered and dressed for the office in one of her favourite dusky pink shirts, which she'd paired with form-fitting, lightly flared dove-grey trousers. The meeting wasn't taking place until late afternoon, but she had some files to prepare and some facts to confirm. Valerio's presence was only a small part of her attack plan. She never walked into anything without considering every possible angle, and today was going to be no different.

The housekeeper showed her out to an impressive marble dining terrace, bathed in golden morning sunshine and surrounded by creeping vines full of beautiful spring wild flowers. Valerio was drinking a steaming cup of coffee and staring blankly out at the hustle of Port Hercules below in the distance. His dark brow was furrowed when he turned to acknowledge her, standing to pull out a chair. She wasn't used to such small, chivalrous gestures. It made her slightly uncomfortable. But she knew he'd been raised in Italian high society—it was likely just second nature.

She avoided his eyes, thanking his house-keeper with a wide smile when she appeared with a platter of fresh fruit and a fresh pot of water for tea before disappearing again.

'I remember you don't drink coffee.' Valerio looked across at her, his eyes slits of stormy blue under his furrowed brow. 'I've had a selection of teas ordered in. I don't know if they're any good.'

'Thank you. That was very thoughtful.'

Dani felt a glow of warmth bloom in her chest, then instinctively pushed it away, remembering that she was trying to keep her guard up. But a small part of her whispered that Valerio had never been purposely unkind to her in the past—only indifferent. It wasn't *his* fault that she'd been attracted to him. If he was trying to make a gesture of goodwill, she should accept it.

She made a show of admiring the fine bone china teapot and selected her favourite brand of English breakfast tea. They passed a few moments in companionable silence, with the buffer of the usual city sounds forming a background.

'We need to discuss our living arrangements,' he said, then waited a moment, frowning at her stunned silence. 'I'm aware that you haven't yet permanently occupied any of the homes that will form your inheritance. My villa is not the most convenient location, but it has a large study you can use for your consulting work.'

Dani felt something tighten in her throat as she looked down at the ring on her left hand. She had been so preoccupied with today's meeting she'd foolishly thought they would just brush past the fact that they were now engaged to be married.

'Valerio…we haven't even talked about the logistics of this arrangement yet and you're already saying you want me to move in here with you?'

'Yes—as soon as possible.' He looked away, his jaw tighter than steel. 'Obviously we won't share a bedroom, but living under one roof will be better for your safety as well as for keeping the appearance of a normal marriage.'

Dani marvelled at the utter madness of his words. 'We both know that there is nothing "normal" about this marriage. But from a PR point of view, I suppose I agree.' She sat back, running a finger along the filigree rim of her teacup. 'I've still got a lease on my apartment in London, but that can be easily fixed. And I won't need your study, as Velamar is my only priority for the time being.'

'Good.' He paused, meeting her eyes as he processed the end of her statement. 'Wait… you've stopped taking on any independent clients? Why would you do that?'

'It's kind of hard to be the sole leader of a global brand and still find time to fly around the world on consulting contracts with unpredictable time frames.' She squared her shoulders. 'I made a conscious choice to focus on Velamar for my own reasons.' She spoke with a clear edge to her tone. 'Just as I will continue to do so now that I'm inheriting the responsibility.'

Valerio pinched the bridge of his nose sharply. 'Dani, I didn't think through leaving you the sole responsibility of Velamar while I was gone. You have to know I would never have allowed you to sacrifice your own career in order to step in for me.'

'Well, then, it's a good thing I didn't need your permission, isn't it?' She cleared her throat, pouring more tea into her cup. 'I'm not here to discuss my career decisions. Please can we just continue with the discussion at hand?'

For a moment he looked as though he fully intended to start an argument. But then he exhaled on a low growling sigh and braced two hands on the balcony ledge. 'We will live here, then, for the time being. For obvious reasons, we will both need to remain unattached while this arrangement is in place. Will that be a problem?'

'*You're* the notorious womaniser.' She raised one brow in challenge. 'If anyone will struggle with discretion, it won't be me.'

He seemed annoyed at her comment, his eyes darkening to a storm. 'I'm not talking about my wife indulging in discreet affairs—I'm talking about you abstaining from them completely. Just as I will.'

She froze at his use of the word 'wife', baffled at the sudden intensity in his gaze and the effect it was having on the knot in her stomach.

She hadn't been trying to insult him—it was no secret that he liked to date a variety of beautiful women. He hadn't been photographed with anyone since the accident, but likely he'd just been discreet. She seriously doubted that his name and the word 'abstinence' had ever been uttered in the same sentence.

'Dani, you know how this needs to look to anyone who is watching. I wish that I could have found any other way...'

'Yes, yes—I get it that you're making a huge sacrifice by marrying me.' She was surprised herself at her own flash of annoyance, and saw his eyes widen in response. Softening her voice a little, she avoided his curious gaze. 'Fine. So I move my stuff in with you and there will be no sordid photographs in the press of me with a string of lovers. Understood.'

'Good.' He was still watching her, his strong, tanned fingers idly twirling a spoon through his second cup of espresso. 'I'm glad we understand each other.'

Dani ignored the flush of awareness that prickled along her skin at the effortlessly sexy tone of his voice. Being around Valerio Marchesi so much was already causing mayhem on her nerves and she was agreeing to *marry* the man? Suddenly she felt caged in by all the unknowns about this arrangement and her ability to survive it.

'Is there a time frame for all of this?' she asked as nonchalantly as she could manage. 'I mean to say…how long do we actually need to stay married?'

His eyes darkened. 'Already dying to be free of me, *tesoro*?'

She inhaled sharply at the endearment, noting that he seemed slightly unnerved by his own words as well. He pulled gently at the collar of his shirt as though it had suddenly grown too tight.

The tense silence between them was interrupted by soft footsteps in the doorway to the kitchen. His housekeeper moved towards them, announcing an urgent phone call from Valerio's brother on the landline.

'Take the call. I've got to get to the office anyway,' Dani urged.

'This conversation is far from over, Dani.' He stood, unbuttoning the top buttons of his shirt. 'I'll pick you up for lunch. You can brief me on the meeting.'

And with a barely audible curse under his breath, he excused himself, disappearing inside with swift, thundering steps.

Dani watched him go with a mixture of relief and disappointment. *'I wish that I could have found any other way.'* Just what every woman wanted to hear from her fiancé. He had sounded as if he was prepping himself for a walk to the gallows.

His brother had probably got wind of the news and was calling now to put a stop to such madness. She shouldn't be hurt by Valerio's coldness. This was business. This was a formal transaction—a professional arrangement and nothing more. From his standpoint this was simple and clear-cut. *He* wasn't tied up in knots by complicated feelings and emotions the way she was.

She thought back to all the times she had dreamed of her own wedding day. She cared little about the actual day itself—more what it represented. Commitment, love, a family of her own and a home filled with happy memories. Deep down she craved the love and devotion she'd seen while growing up.

Her parents had adored one another and had always put their children's welfare before their own. They'd traded in their lofty social scene in Brazil when she was ten years old for a simple life in the English countryside. She had always imagined herself doing the same for her own children some day—that was why she had said yes when her ex, Kitt, had proposed after only six months of dating...even when a small voice in her head had told her to slow down and think it through.

But when her career had skyrocketed, she had realised that the high-powered work life she craved wasn't easily compatible with the traditional family life she had once dreamed of. At least that was what Kitt had said when he'd given her his ultimatum. He'd told her that her ambition and refusal to compromise was ruining any chance they had of a future.

Maybe this kind of business arrangement was the closest thing she would ever get to a real marriage. Maybe it was time she faced the fact that her life was never going to be the stuff of fairy tales and maybe that was okay. She loved her work. She was committed to taking care of the legacy her family had left behind, to doing them all proud.

Faking a happy marriage to a man who would never see her as anything but an obligation was a small price to pay for her safety.

It had to be—she had no other choice.

The rest of her morning was a blur, starting with an unplanned meeting with her regional team about some issues that had arisen with their plans for the Monaco Yacht Show. Usually she didn't enjoy playing CEO at meetings, but for once she threw herself into the role, thankful for a slice of normality.

Work had always been a source of calm for her during times of difficulty. Her parents had taught her the value of hard work, ambition and charity, ensuring that neither of their children became entitled trust fund brats. After Duarte had dropped out of college at nineteen, to live the wild life with Valerio, she had thrown herself into graduating with top honours and had then gone on to do the same in her master's degree in Public Relations and Strategic Communications.

When their parents had died so suddenly, in that car accident seven years ago, she'd jumped at Duarte's offer to be Velamar's PR and marketing strategist. She had been the one to help them turn their modest success into an empire. She was more than capable of public speaking and turning on the charm but, being naturally introverted, preferred to do her work from the shadows as much as possible. She did not possess her twin's natural ability to attract people to her with an almost gravitational pull. Duarte had been the wall she had always leaned on and hid behind.

Pushing away the overwhelming sorrow that always accompanied any memory of her twin, she threw herself into a few hours of preparation for the meeting that lay ahead, praying that Valerio would have the good sense to arrive early so that she could prepare him.

But afternoon came without him and she made her way alone to the large boardroom on the top floor of the building, frowning at the eerily empty space. Even the surrounding offices were empty. A feeling of unease crept into her stomach as she tapped a button on her phone, calling her personal assistant.

'Dani, thank God you called. I just saw one of the secretaries for two of the board members…' The young woman gasped, as though she'd been running.

'Are you okay? What's wrong?'

'They moved the meeting!' her PA exclaimed.

'They moved it to Valerio Marchesi's villa and de-liberately chose not to pass on the memo to you.'

Dani felt her fist tighten on the phone until she heard a crunch. Thanking her overwrought PA, she slammed the device down on the table.

He'd moved the meeting and hadn't called her. Damn him.

She had asked him to do one thing—one simple favour... But, as usual, Valerio Marchesi did what he wanted to do and only ever on his own terms. Heaven forbid the man should ever take her advice or think of someone other than himself.

She wanted to fight—she needed a win of some sort. Maybe then she might start to feel something again other than this restless void of work and sleep.

Embracing the hum of adrenaline in her veins, she raced towards the elevators.

Valerio sat at the top of the long marble din-ing table and surveyed the six men and three women seated around him. He told himself that he'd chosen to change the location of the meet-ing to his own home at the last minute because it would give him an advantage—not because he needed the option of retreat if he lost control. And he knew the board members wouldn't be able to resist the chance to find out where he'd disappeared to. To discover if the rumours of his madness were true.

Just to keep a little mystery on his side, he'd spoken very little as they'd commenced their professionally catered lunch, and had given short, clipped answers to their many questions. But his unease had grown as the minutes had turned into an hour and there had been no sign of his fiancée.

Daniela was never late.

He wanted a single-minded focus on finding out who had pushed for Duarte's death certificate, but now he could hardly concentrate.

After ordering one of his guards to find out where she was, he sat back and tried to focus his anger on discovering which of these people, with their greed and lack of patience, had put Dani in danger.

But of course no one else knew the truth behind the seemingly random events that had transpired in Brazil. No one who was still alive, anyway.

Angelus Fiero stood up from his seat near the top of the table, slicking back the neatly oiled salt-and-pepper hair atop his head. Valerio had never met the man in person before last night…

'Marchesi, I'm afraid my flight plans have changed and I need to leave. I'm needed back in Rio sooner than I thought. But I believe I speak for all of us when I say that I'm very relieved to see you return to work.'

Valerio swallowed his final mouthful of crème brûlée, narrowing his eyes at the man with barely restrained menace. Around him, the other board members continued in their heated discussion about the success of their new Fort Lauderdale headquarters and their expansion throughout the Caribbean and South America.

Angelus Fiero had been their very first investor, back when they had started up and had needed capital to bulk up their fleet offerings. An old friend of the Avelar family, he had been trusted with managing the family's affairs in Brazil after their move to England.

'Please, allow me to see you out.'

Valerio stood, prowling slowly beside the table until he stood so close to the other man he could see a tiny vein throbbing at his temple. He had amassed enough experience over the past six months to know when someone wasn't telling the full truth.

As they walked side by side towards the entrance hall, Fiero made small talk about the latest yacht designs. Valerio barely heard a word—he was too busy mentally cataloguing what he knew of the man's character. He had briefly suspected Fiero's involvement in the kidnap after he'd returned from Brazil and started his investigations, but he hadn't found a single motive or link. The man was comfortably wealthy, he had no debts or enemies, and he didn't stand to gain anything from Duarte's death other than the headache of managing the company's reputation and a slew of uneasy investors.

'I was surprised that Daniela didn't join us for lunch today.' Fiero paused in the hallway to don his coat and hat. 'She has to know that half of the board are pushing to have her voted out.'

'Quite a stupid move on their part,' Valerio drawled, 'considering Daniela is about to become officially one of the wealthiest women in Europe, thanks to an anonymous push for Duarte's death certificate to be released. *You* wouldn't happen to know anything about that, would you?'

Another man might have missed the sudden flicker in Fiero's pale blue eyes. He masked it well, subtly clearing his throat and pasting a grimace on his face.

'You should direct your suspicions elsewhere,' he said. 'I've been a good friend to this family.' He shook his head in a perfect show of grief, placing one hand on his chest, where a small gold cross lay over his tie. 'I have information that the death certificate is to be issued at the start of next week. Quite unusual, considering they never recovered the body…did they?'

Valerio felt his fists tighten, and nausea hit his stomach as memories threatened to overcome him. The old man knew something—he could tell by the way he narrowed his eyes, tapping lightly on his hat as he moved towards the door. There was no way to know if he was on the right track, but it was enough for him to place Fiero firmly back on the list of those possibly involved.

He said goodbye to his newly reinstated suspect, closed the door and took in the violent tremor in his hands that had already begun to creep up his forearms at two words. *The body*. The memories were coming hard and fast. The sharp smell of gunpowder was in the air… Blood soaked the ground around his feet.

He swore he could feel every pump of blood in his chest as he started walking, counting backwards from one hundred. He never knew when one of these bouts of dream-like panic would hit, and he'd long ago stopped trying to fight them off or cure them with whisky. Like his scars, he felt they were a permanent part of him.

He reached the nearest bathroom quickly, slamming the door shut just as black spots swam in his vision and forced him to his knees.

CHAPTER SIX

DANI SANK BACK into the alcove under the steps up to Valerio's impressive villa and cursed under her breath. Angelus Fiero had just disappeared into a sleek black car and driven off— which meant she'd likely missed her chance to talk to him. The rest of the board would still be inside, though. Likely being entertained by their prodigal playboy CEO.

Adrenaline fuelling her, she barely waited for the door to be opened by a member of staff before moving quickly through the house, following the sound of raised voices. At a set of large double doors, she paused, pressing her ear against the wood.

'I'm just saying the majority of our clients are male,' someone was saying loudly. 'They flock to us for the promise of the brand. The iconic image of two powerful, handsome playboys who never settle for less than the best.'

'Duarte and Valerio were the dream team...'

A strong female voice sounded out above the others. 'I can't help but feel that Duarte's sister's talents are better kept…behind the curtain, you know?'

'We can't dispute the effectiveness of her marketing strategies—she's had some great ideas,' someone chided gently from further back in the room.

'Yes, but what good are ideas in a company figurehead when she has all the charisma of a wet blanket. She's *boring*,' a male voice sneered, inciting a rumble of laughter that Dani felt pierce through the thin layer of bravado she'd arrived with.

Any belief she'd held on to that only a small portion of the board wanted her gone instantly disappeared. She felt her cheeks heat, her heart rate speeding up in the uncomfortable way she knew all too well. Old scars burst open. Damn them for making her feel this way. Damn them for seeing her brother as perfect and her as a poor replacement.

Someone cleared his throat behind her, making her almost jump out of her skin.

'Eavesdropping, are we?'

Valerio stood braced against a door frame on the other side of the hall—how long he'd been standing behind her was anyone's guess.

She straightened, rubbing her palms on the

front of her trousers. 'It's impossible to eaves-drop on a meeting I am entitled to attend.'

'I had the notification of the change in venue sent hours ago. It's not my fault you're late.' He glowered down at her, the expression on his face strangely blank, his eyes unfocused.

'Well, that "notification" was purposely kept from me.' She moved to sidestep him, only to have him hold on to her elbow and gently ma-noeuvre her back.

Something wasn't right, she realised. He seemed on edge. There was a sheen of sweat on his brow and he was just a little paler than his usual olive tone. She stopped herself from enquiring, though, remembering how defensive he had been about his behaviour that morning.

Her pulse skipped a little as she looked back towards the door, feeling dread creep in at the thought of walking in and facing those men and women after hearing what they really thought of her.

Valerio tipped his head slightly, listening to the voices still perfectly audible through the door.

'Daniela Avelar is not his usual type.' A man laughed. 'She's frumpy and she frowns too much. No sex appeal, you know?'

'He may be marrying her, but we need to make it clear that Marchesi alone as CEO is our best move forward,' someone else said, inciting a loud murmur of assent from the others.

Dani felt Valerio stiffen beside her, heard a shallow gust of breath leaving his lungs. Mortification threatened to overcome her, but she stood strong, plastering a smirk on her face as she turned to face him with a shrug.

'They've been singing my praises, as you can hear. Clearly they *adore* me.'

'Lose the sarcasm,' he gritted out, bracing one large hand on the door frame. Tension filled his powerful body, as though he were suddenly poised for battle. 'I'll put an end to this. I won't allow them to discuss you this way.'

'You assume that I plan to just walk away?' She raised one brow, stepping past him and inhaling a deep, fortifying breath. She disliked confrontation, but that didn't mean she was incapable of fighting her own battles.

Without warning, she slammed the door open and strode into the room, leaving Valerio momentarily frozen in the doorway behind her.

'Someone forgot to invite the boring temporary CEO to lunch, it seems.' She threw a glance around as she took a seat at the head of the table and folded her arms across her chest.

Multiple pairs of eyes landed on her, widening. Some looked down at the remnants of their coffee, spread out on the dining table along with their files and spreadsheets.

'I'd like to know who kept the change of venue from me.' She spoke with calm assertion, narrowing her eyes as one of the men cleared his throat and sat forward.

'Miss Avelar, there must be some mistake...'

'There have been many mistakes made.' Dani shook her head, pursing her lips. 'Shall I begin listing them?'

She slid a folder from her briefcase, opening up the file she'd prepared in advance the moment she'd realised a coup was in the works. She had evidence here to remove at least four board members for a variety of infractions that violated the company's code of ethics. And as she read out her first statement, the room was completely silent.

Footsteps sounded from the doorway. Daniela paused for a moment, watching as the man most of them truly wanted as their CEO finally entered the room. All eyes shifted to him, as if silently begging him to intervene, to stop this woman from tearing apart their plans.

Dani swallowed hard as his eyes met hers across the room. The impressive expanse of his shoulders was showcased in a simple white shirt with an open collar. She felt a thoroughly inappropriate flash of lust and instantly chided herself. He *had* to know how impressive he looked, damn him. He wouldn't look out of place on a Parisian runway. She knew that her larger frame would *never* be compared to a supermodel, but she certainly wasn't frumpy.

She waited a heartbeat as he silently took a seat at the opposite end of the table, but instead of cutting short her speech, he simply nodded and motioned for her to continue.

A gruelling hour followed, during which four members of the board were put on temporary suspension and the table became filled with more tension than ever. Dani handed out sheets advising some further steps she wished to take regarding the future management of their design branches and charity assets, but decided to leave the actual decision making to a future meeting. Slow and steady was sometimes the best course of action.

Valerio had been reserved throughout the whole process, only answering when directly spoken to. A strange tension seemed to emanate from him, and every now and then she caught his eyes on her, burning with something dark and unrecognisable. Uncomfortable, she lost a little steam towards the end of her speech, and was almost relieved when he finally spoke up and commanded the room.

'I'd like to address some of the comments I

have overheard,' he said. He spoke calmly, but with a gravelly hardness to his tone. 'Firstly, our brand is based on experience, reliability and being ahead of the market—not on a room full of aging business execs who have an opinion on the sex appeal or charisma of those who lead it. Secondly, you will not pass further comment on the details of my relationship with my future wife or debate the reasoning for our marriage. She may be graceful enough not to retaliate against such nonsense, but I am not bound by the same brand of polite restraint.'

Dani shivered as his eyes met hers for a split second.

Exhausted, she was relieved when Valerio began to take charge of escorting the others out. She walked over to the large windows and caught sight of her reflection in the glass. Her trousers were wrinkled and her wild curls seemed to have grown even wilder than usual, but she didn't care. She felt powerful after the surprising success of the afternoon, despite the awful comments she'd overheard.

It seemed like a lifetime ago that she had spent so much of her energy trying to reduce her curves and bumps, trying to squeeze into waist-slimming corsets and spending hundreds of euros on having her thick Latina curls chemically straightened. She'd been obsessed with looking like the hordes of slimmer business-women with their designer suits and pin straight styling.

After her failed almost-jaunt down the aisle and subsequent break-up with Kitt, something had clicked inside her and she'd started working to accept the body she had. The one she'd been born with. She was done with being shamed.

Valerio returned to the room, closing the door behind him with purpose. Evidently the meeting was not entirely concluded. She sat down again.

'That was very well done,' he said sincerely, bracing his hands on the dining table. 'But it makes what I'm about to say even more difficult.'

She froze, taking in the darkness of his eyes, and felt trepidation churn in her gut.

'I'll be stepping back into my role as CEO of Velamar and I want you to take a step back. Maybe recommence your plans to start up your own firm.'

Stunned, she met his eyes. 'What the—?'

'I asked you to trust me.' His voice was sincere. 'I need you to take a step back from the spotlight for a while…until I have a few things in order.'

'You mean you don't want me leading the brand either? What a shocker.' She fought the urge to slam her hand down on the table. 'I will not allow you to put my brother's legacy at risk with your own shallow prejudice.'

'*My* prejudice?' His brows knitted together. 'They're the ones with ridiculous closed ideas of sex appeal and whatever else. I defended you.'

'You might as well have agreed with them. You're doing exactly what they want—getting me out of the picture so they can start picking this company apart like a damn chicken bone. You can't do this.'

In one single sentence he'd washed away all her self-doubt and made her feel appreciated for her talent. And then he'd ruined it all by railroading over her authority and making decisions for her once again.

'I can.' He stood slowly, stalking towards her like a predator. 'I am the only legal chief executive of this company. I appointed you as temporary CEO in my absence and I have the power to revoke that appointment.'

'You. Bastard.' She stood her ground even as he towered over her.

'Perhaps.' He shrugged. 'But if you trusted me you'd believe me when I say I have my reasons.'

He allowed his gaze to wander down her face…and further. She felt the heat of his eyes sweep along her chest and abdomen, right down to her toes. She took a step back, the urge overpowering her.

'If you think I agree with any of the things they said about you and your…assets… Clearly you have no idea what the meaning of sex appeal is, either.'

Her breath caught in her throat. Her mind was whirring, trying to find a clever retort to his words. He had to be trying to unnerve her, to make her leave. She felt hot shame rise within her, along with that damn pulse of awareness that refused to leave her every time he was in her vicinity. He was a beacon of sexual energy and, like a pathetic moth to his flame, she was completely unable to stay away.

'I've just been informed that Duarte's death will be certified in a matter of days,' he said. 'We don't have time for this back and forth.' He reached for the remnants of his coffee, downing the last of the liquid with a hiss of satisfaction. 'I need our marriage taken care of and tied up legally before your inheritance is unlocked. We could be married in St Lucia by Monday morning if we leave tonight.'

'St Lucia?' She repeated the words slowly, her shoulders tensing as she began to prepare all the reasons why she couldn't just up and disappear to the Caribbean without making plans for the business.

Then she remembered he'd technically just fired her from the only job she currently had. She had no reason not to go.

'I'm not your enemy, you know.' He spoke softly.

'I know.' She sighed. 'Right, I guess we're eloping, then.' She made a weak attempt at a smile. 'We've got a new base being built there. I've been monitoring the building work remotely, via our management team on the ground, but I'd love the chance to go and do a walk-through.'

'Should I be offended that your first thought is how to turn our romantic Caribbean wedding into a chance to get some work done?' He seemed irritated, gathering papers from the table and then thrusting them back down with a huff of breath.

'It's not a wedding,' she said quickly, frowning at his strange change in mood. 'It's an elopement. I don't understand why you're on edge—snapping as though you're angry with me for all this.'

'I'm not angry with you, Dani...' he growled, turning to walk towards the door. 'I'm angry that you've been put in this situation. And I'm angry that you still refuse to trust me. But really I'm always on edge—so maybe you'd best get used to that.'

* * *

Valerio had just ended a painful phone call with his mother—his second family intervention of the day—when their car arrived on the runway beside the sleek Marchesi family jet. He felt a nervous twitch in his stomach as he watched Dani walk across the Tarmac ahead of him, in her perfect form-fitting trousers and flowy blouse.

She was polite, greeting the in-flight attendant as she stowed their bags and accepted some light refreshments. He gestured to the seat across from him and noticed her face tighten as she moved into it, her posture screaming with tension.

Just as he planned to apologise for his abrupt behaviour after their meeting, his phone rang again.

Seeing his brother's name show up on the display, he cursed aloud and jammed his finger on the screen to block the call. Ramming one hand through his hair, he closed his eyes and huffed out a loud breath filled with frustration.

'Is there a problem?' his fiancée enquired with a raised brow.

For a moment he considered not answering her question at all. But then he remembered the promise he'd made to himself as they'd driven in silence to the airport—to at least *try* not to be so closed off and abrasive with her. She was going to be his wife… They were going to be sharing a lot more time together. He needed to put some effort in to his behaviour.

Reluctantly, he sat down across from her and met her eyes. 'You saw that I got a call from my brother earlier today, followed quickly by one from my mother? We haven't been on the best terms since I came back from Brazil. I've been distant, and now they've found out about our engagement through the media… Needless to say, my family are not happy about our elopement plans.'

Dani frowned. 'Of course they're not. I never even thought of how they might see this. Do they know all the details?'

He frowned. 'My brother knows a bit, but I've told him not to tell our parents the full truth. I can't tell them about the danger, not when my mother is such a worrier. They think it's a real marriage.'

He thought back to the sound of worry in his brother's voice on the phone. Rigo Marchesi had never been one to give his little brother an easy time, but after the display Valerio had put on at that christening dinner… Well, he couldn't remember all the details, but he was pretty sure that he deserved the scorn in his brother's voice. His entire family had believed him dead for two

weeks and had been overjoyed at his return—
only to be shut out and ignored for months on
end.

They didn't realise that it was better this way.

'I won't pretend to understand what you've
been working through these past months,
fratello,' Rigo had said, 'but this seems quite
sudden. I've been around you and Dani many
times. She hates your guts and she is possibly
the only woman I've ever witnessed being utterly immune to your charms.'

'No one is immune to my charms.' Valerio
had answered easily. 'It's not like that. It's more
like a business arrangement between us.'

'Now, where have I heard that before…?'
Rigo had laughed out loud.

Rigo and his wife, Nicole, had married years
before, as the result of a media scandal. Rigo
had sworn his marriage was in name only, and
yet now they were the picture of married bliss,
with two small daughters and another on the
way.

Across from him, Dani cleared her throat,
pulling him back to the present. 'Valerio, if this
is causing problems for your family, we should
find another way. We can find someone with
similar financial power and influence that we
can trust.'

'Someone like Tristan Falco?' The venom-filled words were out of his mouth before he could stop them.

'I wasn't thinking of Tristan, but now that you say it, he might be a good fit.'

Valerio tensed. *Over his dead body.*

'I wouldn't trust anyone else—and neither should you. My family will get over it.'

He stood up, stretching his lower back muscles and pouring himself a glass of cold water to try to calm his nerves.

He had to admit that not once had he thought of his parents' reaction to his sudden nuptials. Amerigo and Renata Marchesi were not fiercely traditional, and they had always pushed their sons to choose their own path in life. But his mother was understandably hurt.

Once again he was a disappointment. Even when for once he was being selfless in his actions. He had nothing to gain from shackling himself in marriage other than protecting Daniela from harm and fulfilling his promise to her brother.

A small part of him spoke up, pointing out that so far he seemed to have been a lot more preoccupied with their living situation and ensuring she was by his side. He should have been working more on investigating possible perpetrators—like Fiero.

He leaned down, pinching the bridge of his

nose sharply. '*Dio*, why is everything so damn complicated?'

Truthfully, he'd been relieved to talk things through with his older brother earlier. Rigo had been by his side at every important moment in his life—the day he'd dropped out of college, the day he'd told his father that he didn't want to be a part of the family business, and the day he'd cut the ribbon on the first company premises. Rigo had always offered impartial advice and support. He had always been a rock no matter how heavy the storm.

But his father was another story. Amerigo Marchesi had always hoped his two sons would run the family business together, but Valerio had never coped well behind a desk. He had been a wild teenager and an even wilder adult, taking on whatever ridiculous challenges life threw at him. He had once thrived on adrenaline and risk—now he spent his days obsessing over one woman's safety. The irony was not lost on him...

When Dani suggested they talk through some of the details of the new base they were going to visit in St Lucia, he jumped at the chance to shut his brain off by listening to the progress she'd made on the project. It was impressive—more impressive than anything he and Duarte could have planned. She was a marvel at organising, and seeing details no one else did.

When she finally yawned, and said she was going to try to sleep for the rest of the flight, he almost asked her to stay and tell him more. Something about her presence soothed him and made him feel less adrift. But in the end he let her go with a single nod.

Once he was alone he felt a familiar restlessness settling into his bones. The last time he'd been in St Lucia had been a few days before the accident with Duarte. They had been finalising the purchase of their new premises there when Duarte had told him that he needed to go to Brazil for a couple of days to sort out some business. At the last minute Valerio had decided to follow him as a surprise, so they could celebrate their expansion plans.

Valerio tried in vain to shut himself off to the memory…tried to block out the anger and regret. He'd spent months torturing himself for not realising that something was up with his best friend, that the man had been preoccupied and taking mysterious phone calls in the middle of important meetings. He'd clearly been under some unseen pressure, but Valerio had believed his excuse that he was just 'in a situation' with a woman.

Duarte had been an intense guy at the best

of times—it had been easier for Valerio to look away and focus on growing their empire.

Regret washed over him, and once again he fought the urge to ask his fiancée to come back and discuss more business plans. She would likely jump at the chance. She loved to talk about work, and he could simply lose himself in her soothing presence.

Then he cursed himself for his own selfishness, hoping he might relax enough to sleep but knowing it was completely hopeless that he would ever feel at rest.

When Dani awoke, a number of hours later, she found Valerio sleeping soundly on his recliner in the main cabin. She walked over to stand beside him, fighting the urge to cover him with a blanket. He had told her never to touch him while he slept and she wasn't about to overstep that boundary, no matter how much she wanted to soothe the beast that roared in him.

Frowning, she took a seat at the opposite end of the cabin and successfully busied her fretful mind by reading over some of the finer details of their new Caribbean expansion. She might not be a fully active CEO, thanks to his demotion of her, but she had been the one to put the work into the planning of this base and she wasn't about to let him go in unprepared. She was able to separate her emotions from her professional work.

She thought of Valerio's urging her to focus on her independent contracts and how success had felt when it had been on her own terms. It had been hard work, a lot of travelling, and impossible to forge any kind of relationship in such a transient role. But that was what had drawn her to the work in the beginning—it had been the perfect balance. She had spent half her time working with her brother and the other half travelling solo.

But even though she had believed she was content, something had felt strangely lacking. The travel had grated on her sleep schedule, and she'd felt no desire to see any of the cities she'd landed in, preferring just to get her work done and sit in her rented apartment or hotel room watching romantic comedies and eating cold pizza from the box.

The lack of travel in the past six months while she had been running Velamar had been a welcome change of pace, but it still hadn't quite eased the restlessness that had long plagued her.

In the months before Duarte's death, she had been drawing up plans to start her own PR firm—something she had always dreamed of. Initially she had believed that she needed more experience or larger jobs—that no one would take her seriously until she had proved herself on a grand scale. But bigger jobs and more respect had come and still she'd held back.

Now she was about to be the co-owner of a global yacht charter firm and about to marry her business partner.

Unable to focus on work any more, she set about tidying away the items that Valerio had left out on the table. A photograph slid from his wallet onto the floor and she picked it up, frowning as an image including herself stared back at her. She remembered that day. The picture had been taken at the very first charity yacht gala she had planned six years ago. Just a few months before she'd moved to London and met Kitt.

Duarte stood centre stage, looking straight into the camera, while Dani and Valerio stood either side of him. Dani's hand was outstretched towards her brother's best friend as though she was mid-punch. She sighed, seeing that look in her eyes that she remembered so well. But she couldn't quite place the expression on Valerio's face…

Embarrassment, perhaps?

Had she been that obvious?

She scrunched her face up, cursing how terrible she had always been at disguising her emotions. Even now, did he know how utterly infatuated she had been with him? Could he tell that she still struggled with that pull of attraction?

She let her eyes wander from the photograph to the real-life, grown-up version of the man. He lay completely relaxed, his strong jaw in profile, showcasing the kind of chiselled designer stubble that most male models would have killed for. His arms were crossed over his broad chest, where the material of his shirt strained over the taut muscles that lay underneath.

She imagined what this flight might have been like had they been a real engaged couple on their way to a romantic whirlwind elopement. That version of her wouldn't have thought twice about sliding onto her sleeping fiancé's lap and running her fingers along his perfect jaw to wake him with a sizzling kiss... And maybe that kiss would have led to the kind of mile-high aeroplane chair sex she had only ever read about in magazine confession columns.

Just as she allowed herself to imagine the mechanics of such an act, the Captain chose to announce their descent. Valerio woke with his familiar knee-jerk rapid awareness. His eyes landed on her and Dani felt herself freeze as though she'd been caught with her hand in the proverbial cookie jar.

His gaze seemed curious, and she wondered

if her erotic daydreams were somehow painted across her forehead. She felt far too warm as she cleared her throat and slid into the seat across from him, averting her gaze as she commented all too loudly on the picture-perfect view of the island of St Lucia below.

Their first stop was the office of a very prestigious local attorney, to ensure that the documents their company lawyer had filed in application for a marriage licence had been received. They were assured that all was going to plan, and that the short ceremony would take place in two days' time, as per the legal waiting period during which they must not vacate the island.

Dani ignored the twist of nerves in her gut at the idea that in a mere forty-eight hours she would be legally wed to the silently brooding man by her side. He had been distant since their argument, his brow permanently marred by that single worry line in the centre. At one point she had almost reached out to smooth it down—had even had to pull her hand into a tight fist and marvel at how ridiculous she was being.

They left the attorney's office and walked the short distance to the marina, where Velamar's sleek new Caribbean base was in the final stages of being finished. The building was single-storey, in traditional St Lucian style, with an enviable frontage of the large marina, which housed the beginnings of their sleek new fleet of charter yachts and catamarans.

'Well, what do you think?'

Dani crossed her arms as Valerio silently took in the bright, modern entrance foyer. The interior was still a mess of plastic coverings and unfinished paintwork, but the majority of the structural modifications had been completed exactly according to her orders.

Valerio was silent, his eyes seeming to take in every small detail as he moved around the large space. He craned his neck upwards to the feature chandelier hanging above their heads and let out a low whistle.

'I had it commissioned by a local artist.' Dani spoke quickly, before he tried to comment on the possible price of such a frivolous item. 'I used local tradesmen for everything—including furniture design. I figured it was good for our global image, as well as making a statement about our commitment to being a part of this community—not just another big company setting up shop.'

'It's genius. This design is the perfect blend of our brand mixed with a St Lucian flavour.' He shook his head. 'You're perfectly on schedule too, by the looks of things. We've never managed that on any of our projects before.'

She fought the impulse to make a snarky comment about how she *was* just that good—about how he was making a mistake by removing her from her CEO duties. Instead she let his compliment sit for a moment, then replied with a simple thank-you. It was very adult, for the pair of them. Very professional.

More than once she caught him watching her from the corner of her eye as she spoke to the small management team who had been running things on-site. They were jumping over one another, eager to show the progress that had been made in readying the base for the first launch in the upcoming season.

Valerio seemed oddly distant now, allowing her to take the lead on the walk-through while he stood to the side and listened.

She suggested they take the team to dinner, to show their appreciation of their hard work, and was delighted when Valerio booked a sleek little boutique restaurant on the harbour that served the most delicious lobster she had ever tasted. He stepped easily into the role of charming CEO as he regaled the small table with entertaining stories from the company's early days, starting up in Monaco, and the various catastrophes they had endured.

She felt an enormous sense of pride in her company—and then froze, wondering when on earth she had begun thinking of it as hers and not Duarte's. It was as if hearing that his death was about to be confirmed had forced her to start accepting that he was not coming back to claim what should have always been his.

She found herself struggling to keep up with the jovial conversation during the rest of dinner, and fell into silence on the short drive up the coast to the villa Valerio had leased for the weekend.

It was nestled high on the side of a hill in a small inlet, with a short private beach visible between the cliffs below. The house itself was a warm peach-coloured creation of concrete and salvaged wood, surrounded by beautiful potted trees. Wild flowers grew up its façade, along with green foliage along the windows.

She stepped out of the car, breathing in the warm sea breeze. There wasn't a sound around them other than the chirping of birds and the muted crash of the waves on the wind. It took her breath away. It was as if her own personal postcard fantasy of an island paradise had been dreamed into life.

But even such a spectacular panorama couldn't cut through the heavy cloud that had come over her. Grief was a strange thing. It seemed to disappear then pop back up when you least expected it.

She followed Valerio as he led the way past the front door, following a lamplit paved path around the side of the house. The manicured gardens stretched for what seemed like miles around them, sloping gently down towards a sharp cliff edge. Whoever had designed this space had ensured a perfect symmetry between the smooth curving lines of the house and the natural beauty of the landscape.

Her heart felt both happy and sad as she inwardly acknowledged that her brother would have loved it.

'This place is magical,' she breathed softly as she wandered around to a sprawling terrace at the rear of the villa, which stretched out from the cliff face on what seemed like stilts, dug down into the rock itself. It was quite literally as if you could walk right out into the clouds from here.

At this northernmost point of the island, the Caribbean stretched out endlessly to one side, the Atlantic Ocean in the distance on the other. On a clear day, she'd bet you could see all the way to the neighbouring island of Martinique.

'I'm glad you like it.' Valerio had a smile in his voice as he spoke, stopping at the polished wooden balustrade beside her. 'I was thinking that, instead of the courthouse, we could just get married right here.' When she was utterly silent, he continued awkwardly. 'I have my security team on-site… It would be easier to contain. Plus, I thought it might be a bit of a nicer view than stacks of paperwork and musty bookshelves.'

Dani felt every romantic cell in her body light up from the inside out, the idea of saying her vows in such a place making her eyes water. But then she remembered that they weren't real vows, and that she wasn't to be a real bride in this picture-perfect setting. That the reason he had to keep her safe was because someone wanted to hurt her.

She felt herself deflate like a helium balloon coming down from the heavens. As beautiful as this place was, no amount of dressing it up would make this wedding any less painful.

CHAPTER SEVEN

VALERIO WAS PUZZLED by the sudden change in Dani as she simply nodded and murmured something non-committal about his idea sounding 'nice'. He pursed his lips, ignoring the sinking disappointment in his gut at her reaction.

He wasn't sure why he'd hoped she would be happy with the setting—they both knew that this was just a quick formality that needed to be done. It really didn't matter if they signed their licence and said their vows by the side of a road—only that the legalities were seen to.

He watched as she wandered down the terrace, briefly taking in the impressive pool area, then moved inside the house to explore. Valerio kept a few steps behind her as she looked around, commenting on the vibrant colours of the potted plants and the flowers around each room. For the most part, the rented house was decorated in neutral tones of white and grey. It was lacking an owner's touch of personality.

The kitchen looked like a relatively new addition, as did the state-of-the-art surveillance system and security room. The privacy and safety of the house had been one of Valerio's main concerns when booking, and he had advised his two guards to take shifts in the guest cabin at the gate. He wasn't going to take any chances.

'I'm going to go unpack my stuff…maybe take a shower.'

She wandered away through the house and Valerio watched her go, a feeling of unease within him. She was unhappy—he had seen it in the set of her mouth all the way through dinner. He had respected her silence in the car with difficulty, wanting to give her space in whatever bothered her, but he had also wanted to stop the car and demand she tell him what was wrong.

But it wasn't his place. He wasn't the man for her to confide her innermost feelings to…to lean on when she was sad. If he started blurring those lines, who knew what would come falling down next? Distance wasn't just wise with Dani; it was absolutely necessary.

Ignoring the sudden increase of tension in his spine, he moved to the fridge and found it fully stocked, as requested. Fresh fruit and pre-cooked gourmet meals lined the shelves— enough to keep them going for a couple of days while they waited for the paperwork to go through.

Suddenly, the idea of sitting around waiting for the formalities of their elopement just didn't sit right with him. If they had any hope of making this work, they needed to get back on the same team. He needed her to trust him, and not to feel like a coiled spring in his company.

Suddenly, he knew exactly what to do.

The tiny beach restaurant was a hidden gem Valerio had heard about on the east side of the island. Dani had initially worried aloud that her simple turquoise shift dress might make her feel underdressed, but that had been before Valerio had revealed that he'd booked out the entire venue for their exclusive use.

'There's no one else here,' she whispered as they were seated at a small table overlooking a pebbled beach. Small lanterns lit the way down to the shore and a light scent of salt was in the cool night air. 'I understand we need to be cautious, but it's so quiet.'

He nodded towards an area at the edge of the deck and watched as she turned and saw the duo of island musicians setting up under a string of fairy lights. Soon the sound of a steel drum and a rhythmic guitar began to flow through the air. She smiled as she closed her eyes and swayed a little.

'You should do that more often,' Valerio said silkily, taking a sip of his soda water and lime to distract himself from the hum of attraction that had refused to shift since she'd walked down the stairs in that flowy knee-length dress. She shifted and crossed one leg over the other, revealing a long, smooth expanse of perfectly curved skin. He cleared his throat, looking up to her face and away from those damn thighs. 'I want you to enjoy these few days here. Take it as a chance to recharge before we have to return to reality.'

'Or at least the new appearance of reality.' She smiled again.

'Exactly.'

The corners of his mouth tipped up slightly and for the first time he felt the urge to laugh. It was enough to stop him for a moment, before he caught himself. He'd had a hard time too, he reminded himself. Maybe they both deserved to feel a little freedom while they were here.

'You're starting to look serious again,' she commented, one brow raised.

'I was just thinking…maybe it's time we called a truce. Let's enjoy a few days off the grid, so to speak. No arguments or work. No serious talk.'

A simple handshake sealed the deal and they entered into a pleasant flow of conversation until their food arrived then drifted into companionable silence as the delicious food and great music added to their lighter mood.

Their waiter was a kind-faced older man, who saw the ring on Daniela's finger and insisted that the band play a slow number for them to dance to.

Valerio stood, extending his hand to her and forcing a smile as she stood up and moved close. The music had a soft, seductive rhythm, and he found himself forgetting all the reasons why he shouldn't be enjoying this, why he shouldn't pull her close and pretend they were just another couple on an island adventure.

He breathed in the scent of her hair and heard the softest sigh escape her lips.

'I didn't expect you to be a good dancer.' She spoke near his ear, her breath fanning his skin. 'I should have known you'd be good at everything.'

'You think I find everything easy?' He subtly moved even closer, moving his hand on her back and leaning forward. 'I stepped on every dance partner's toes at events when I was a teenager. My mother made me go to dance lessons twice a week for six months. I was an embarrassment.'

She laughed deep in her throat as he dipped

her into a flamenco-style twirl, tipping her back over his arm. 'Well, you certainly overcame your awkward phase.'

Their eyes met for a long moment, their breath coming a little faster from their exertions. Valerio found himself wondering if he should suggest they kiss, to maintain the appearance of being a happily engaged couple. But really he just wanted to kiss her again. Wanted to see if it was his sex-starved brain that had elicited that first reaction from him after their first kiss or…if it was just simply her.

As he began tipping his head down towards her, a shout from behind them caught his attention.

They both turned and watched as one of the security guards ran down the beach and into the water towards a small boat. A single man was in the vessel, a black boxlike item in his hands. Valerio turned himself in front of Dani, shielding her with his body as he shouted for the other guard to follow.

After a few tense moments of shouting and confusion, it was revealed that the man was just a local fisherman who hadn't been told of the restaurant's private hire. The guards and Valerio quickly apologised to the man, and to the restaurant owner, who had been quite distressed by the commotion.

'Get back to the car,' Valerio growled, guiding her away from the dance floor by the elbow.

'Valerio, it's okay. It was just a mistake.'

'This entire impulsive evening out was a mistake.' He shook his head. 'I can't even keep you safe for one day. I need to get you back to the house now. Just…please don't fight me on this.'

Dani didn't fight him. She barely even spoke on the drive back to the villa, knowing that Valerio needed time to cool down after the adrenaline rush of the false alarm. She had been scared too, but he had moved swiftly from fear and protective mode to anger towards himself. She was beginning to see a pattern with him. Did he have a hero complex? Or was he hiding something about himself?

An email on her phone caught her attention as they entered the large open-plan living area of the villa.

'The board have accepted my plans for Nettuno and the charities.' She frowned. 'But I never got the chance to send them my files before you asked me to step back.'

'I sent them.' He turned to her, both hands in his pockets. 'I looked into your plans further after the meeting and I knew they were the best course of action. You'll get full credit, and I'll keep you in the loop on everything regarding Duarte's projects.'

'Valerio…that means more than you know—thank you.'

'You don't need to thank me. I should be thanking you for being so good at what you do. I'm being honest when I say I wouldn't ask you to take this step back if it wasn't important.'

She nodded once. 'And you still won't tell me exactly why?'

Valerio's gaze became instantly defensive and he prepared to turn away.

'No arguments, remember?' she said quickly, knowing that she needed to take a different tack. This was a business deal, after all—why shouldn't she employ one of her oldest moves? Entertain the opposition…keep them close. 'I'm not going to launch into a fight, if that's what you're thinking. I want us to keep to our deal. A weekend of fun, starting now.'

She moved to one of the sideboards she'd investigated earlier, returning with a deck of cards. 'How do you fancy your odds?'

'Poker?' He raised one brow, picking up the deck and shuffling the cards with seasoned practice. 'You sure you're up to playing me?'

'You forget that I've been schmoozing your clientele in Monte Carlo these past few months. I've become quite a pro.'

'We don't have any chips.'

He shuffled the cards again, dancing them easily between his hands with the lightest touch. She watched his movements, transfixed by how effortlessly he manipulated the deck. The man was good with his hands…

Clearing her wandering thoughts, she sat up straighter. 'I used to play without chips with Hermione back in college. We sat up all night, creating this stupid game where you get a forfeit instead of chips, while we were supposed to be studying for exams.'

'A forfeit?' His eyes met hers across the table. 'Like Truth or Dare?'

'More like Truth or Lies. You have to ask awkward questions and try to get the other person to lie or refuse to answer. But be warned: I'm pretty good at this.'

The premise of the game was simple enough: a crazy mix-up of various card games that only Hermione could have concocted. Each player had the chance to steal cards by challenging the other to answer a question or make a statement, then determining if the answer was the truth or a lie. The problem was, as the game went on for a few rounds, Dani realised that some of the questions Valerio was asking were quite inappropriate.

'How many lovers have you had?' he asked boldly.

Dani answered honestly, praying she didn't blush with embarrassment as she admitted she had only ever been with Kitt. Valerio's eyes burned into hers, widening with disbelief as he declared it a lie, and she shook her head, taking her share of his cards as her forfeit.

'How many lovers have *you* had?' Dani asked when it was her turn, trying and failing to keep a straight face.

Valerio pursed his lips, counting the fingers on both hands, then reaching for a pen and jotting down some sums. 'Let me see. Carry the two...multiply by seven... Roughly in the low hundreds.'

'Okay, well, I'm just going to say that's true.' She shrugged, pretending not to care about his answer.

'Lie.' His eyes sparkled as he took her cards. 'I'm actually quite discerning about who I take to bed, despite the tabloid rumours. You have a low opinion of me.'

Dani smirked. 'Well, what *is* the number, then?'

'Ah-ah, that's not a part of the game.'

He laughed as she groaned her annoyance.

'What's your biggest fear?' he asked on the next turn, his gaze strangely focused on her and a slight curve to his mouth. He was enjoying this, she thought.

'That's an easy one. The open sea,' she said easily, schooling her features.

When he guessed that she was lying, she shook her head, grabbing yet more of his cards.

'You're serious? You work at a yacht charter company and you're afraid of the open sea?' He let out a bark of laughter.

'I'm just afraid of swimming in it—not sailing. I don't like to sail myself, but I trust the boats.'

She sat back as they played another hand, feeling his eyes on her the entire time. The next time her turn came up, she felt the effect of the wine kicking in, along with a new sense of bravado. She asked him some questions about his childhood, his decision not to join his father's company—everything she could think of that she'd always wished to ask.

'What's your most shameful secret?' he asked on his next turn, laughing when she grimaced at his question. 'You know the rules: you have to give an answer or you forfeit.'

'Well, unlucky for you, that's an easy one for me.' She met his gaze, throwing out her best poker face. 'I have never had a proper orgasm.'

His brow furrowed, his eyes narrowing on

her for one intense moment before they widened in a mixture of surprise and anger.

'You have to say if you think it's true or false,' she said, but she was instantly regretting her flirty answer, wondering what on earth had possessed her. 'Or we can just move on.'

The air was still and silent between them, except for the sound of insects chirping and waves crashing against the cliffs nearby. She pursed her lips, sitting up and flicking her hair over her shoulder.

'Forget that one. I'll give you the cards and let's just move on.'

A long exhalation escaped Valerio's lips. Dani looked up to see his hands in tight fists on his lap.

'*Madre di Dio.* I knew that pompous lawyer was beyond useless. You actually believe that you are somehow defective because of that idiot?'

'It's not always the man's fault, Valerio. And it's kind of a sensitive subject,' she said tightly. 'Draw your next hand, please.' She heard the ice in her voice—it was a sore subject for her. But she wasn't about to discuss it over some stupid card game.

'Even if it's true—which is up for debate—you're telling me he made you believe that it was your fault? That you can't—?'

'I said draw your next hand.'

The next round was more heated, with Dani using her best tricks to ensure she won. She knew she was a damn good card player, even if it was an utterly ridiculous game.

She met his eyes across the table. 'Time for your most shameful secret, Mr Marchesi. And it had better match mine.'

Valerio sat back in his seat, still feeling the tension within him from her revelation. He wiped a hand down his face, wishing they'd never started playing this game. She was just giving him as good as she got—she had no idea how many secrets he held in. But she had asked to know before...about Rio. Maybe this was his chance to share his burden with her. He only hoped she would be able to handle it.

'Valerio, you don't have to answer,' she said quickly, obviously taking in the change in him. 'I'll choose a different question.'

'You answered yours,' he said simply. 'I have no problem continuing to play by the rules. My most shameful secret is easy. Most people believe me to be some kind of hero, but the reality is that I'm the opposite. I'm a coward. It was my fault that your brother was killed and I will never forgive myself for that.'

'Valerio...' she breathed.

'No. You asked me for the truth once before, and I walked away. You deserve to know how he died.'

An unbearable pity was there in her deep brown eyes as she nodded once and gestured for him to proceed. He felt her attention on him like the warm heat of the sun, watched her delicate hands folding and unfolding in her lap as she waited. They both knew this wasn't just a game any more.

'I followed him to Rio when he asked me not to. We were attacked by a van full of men and taken,' he began, hearing his own voice sounding out perfectly clear in the night air, as somewhere deep inside his chest ached. 'I woke up in a shipping yard, surrounded by men in black hoods. They roared questions in a Portuguese dialect that I couldn't even begin to understand. Duarte was tied up beside me for a while but then they separated us. They were far more interested in him than me.' In his mind, he remembered the solemn look on Duarte's face as he apologised for dragging him into such a mess… He swore he would get them both freed. That he had a plan, but he made him vow to protect Dani if anything happened to him.

But for days on end they had tortured him and Duarte in turn, in front of each other, never al-

lowing him to speak, only Duarte, using their
loyalty to one another against them.

'Days passed... They tortured me for fun. I
didn't have anything else they needed. I had already offered them money... After they broke
my knee and I could no longer fight back, they
got bored. Then they mostly just left me alone
in the dark.'

He heard a sob and looked up to see that Dani
had covered her face with her hands, but he had
to finish this while he could. He owed her this
story, even if he knew it might break her to hear
it. He hoped she was strong enough.

'Eventually they lost their patience. A man
brought Duarte in and held a gun to my head.
Someone asked in English how much his
friend's life was worth. But one of the guards
who I hadn't seen before turned his gun on the
others. He freed us both before they killed him.
I had a gun in my hand but I hesitated. I had the
chance to end it and I didn't. They shot Duarte
by accident. I saw the panic in their eyes once
they realised. They debated shooting me too
but got disturbed by someone outside and just
knocked me out instead. When I woke up, Duarte's body was gone and so were they.'

Valerio remembered staggering out of that
shipping yard. He was found on the street.
When the police came, they found tracks lead-

ing to the dock—evidence that a body had been dumped in the water. Washed out to sea. They'd dragged his friend's body away, denied him a proper burial.

He shook his head as if coming out of a daze.

'You know the rest.'

He felt a warm weight on the seat beside him and felt himself cocooned in the soft comfort of her intoxicating scent. She leaned her head against his shoulder, her sharp breaths telling him that she was crying even though she hid her face.

'Thank you,' she said simply, and then she allowed the silence to stretch on for a long while. She seemed to know instinctively that he couldn't speak any more, that he needed to just…*be*…for a moment.

No matter how many times he allowed himself to access those memories, they always seemed to hit him with the same force. The look on Duarte's face as he'd realised they weren't getting out of that shipping yard alive. The look of pure hatred in the masked men's eyes as they'd tried again and again to beat him into submission.

Every single moment was like a pinprick in his skin, every vision a reminder of what he might have done differently, how he might have saved his friend's life if he'd not hesitated that split second.

After a long time Dani sat up and turned to him, her eyes a mess of smudged make-up.

'Lie,' she said, an echo to their earlier game.

'Is that your attempt at a joke?'

'I would never joke about what you went through. You came back alive—you survived the unimaginable. But the way you tell that story... It's as though you feel you were to blame for my brother's death. As though you could have saved him if you'd done something different. You're lying to yourself. Punishing yourself for surviving.'

Valerio looked away, his jaw tightening with anger. 'You have no idea what you're talking about.'

'I know that you're a good man. That you would have done what you believed was right. You were under so much pressure—'

'Stop.' He stood up, fury and resentment choking him, making him want to lash out. 'You blame me for his death just as much as everyone else. Are you telling me you have never wondered how I survived when he was clearly the more experienced fighter? You think I don't know what people say about me behind my back? You've had the luxury of grieving him without knowing the details, without having them permanently etched in your memory as a lifelong torture. Do you think you can just pull me out of my life, tie me to a bed and order me to get back to work…go back to living my life? Do you think I can just switch any of this off?'

He laughed, harsh and low.

'I'm done with this game.'

Dani stood up, walking quietly to the door back into the villa. She paused, turning back for a moment to meet his eyes. When she spoke her voice was surprisingly calm and soft in the aftermath of all the venom he'd just thrown at her.

'Valerio… I know you're angry. But there is no luxury in grief, no matter what side you stand on. We both loved him. And I know that I pushed you to come back, but I'm not sorry. I get it that there are parts of you that are broken and scarred from your experience. But I just need you to know that I don't blame you for his death. I never did. And you might have wanted to die in that dark shipping container, but I am thankful every single day that you came back.'

The door to the house closed softly behind her, leaving Valerio to sit alone in the darkness, feeling the result of his own stupid temper and guilt surrounding him like a dark cloud. He took a step forward, willing himself to storm after her and demand that she be angry. Demand the hatred he deserved.

But he remained frozen for a long time, his mind fighting to swim up from the fiery pit of anger it had succumbed to. It was at times like this, when the blackness came over him, when he wondered how there was anything of him left at all.

Valerio kept out of Dani's way the next morning, not even passing comment when she holed herself up in the study at the villa and he spied her hard at work on her computer. She needed to take a break and some time to relax, but she wasn't going to listen to him—not after he had been his usual difficult self last night.

He hardly even remembered half of what he'd said, he'd been so set on telling her the story of what had actually happened in Brazil.

He found his own computer and sat down in the dining room, logging on to the Velamar system for the first time in months and taking in the vast amount of work he'd been neglecting. It was no surprise Dani hadn't had any time for her independent contracts—he'd left her alone to handle all this.

He spent the day through to the afternoon methodically sorting through emails and project outlines, sales projections and marketing plans. He immersed himself in the work, surprised when it fuelled the drive in him rather than making him feel trapped at a desk like it usually did.

His mind felt focused—as if he had unburdened it a little just by sharing his darkness with Dani. But guilt assailed him. He needed to swallow his pride and apologise for his behaviour. For all his behaviour over the past few days. He was about to be her husband, and even if it was in name only, he didn't want to let her down.

'I'm still committed to our agreement of a weekend off, even if you're not. So I'm going to go for a swim before it gets dark.'

Like a mirage, she had appeared in the doorway of the dining room, a towel wrapped around her and the black strings of a simple bikini top visible at her nape.

Cursing himself for his instant flare of arousal, he glared down at his computer, waving a hand in her direction. He listened to her footsteps pad away, closing his eyes at the distinctive sound of a towel hitting a smooth surface before there was the splash of water.

His mind conjured up a vision of her smooth, dark curves gliding through the cool water in the setting sunlight. His groin tightened in response, all the blood in his body rushing south. He snapped the computer shut, looking up at the ceiling and shaking his head. This was what happened when he ignored his body for so long. He was like a teenager around her. She would be horrified to know of his lack of control.

He tried to get back into his work but his concentration was shot. So he sat in painful silence, listening to the sound of her moving through the water on the other side of the terrace doors.

Suddenly a muffled scream came from far away, jolting him from his thoughts. He frowned, tensing. When a second scream sounded out, he jumped from his seat and started running.

He reached the pool to see Daniela frozen in the centre, her eyes wide with terror as she pointed towards the wooden bridge over the water.

He followed her finger, his eyes instantly landing on what was possibly the most gigantic snake he had ever seen. The reptile was olive green in colour, with black markings along its length which almost matched the entire span of the bridge.

As Valerio watched, its heavy body moved and became partially submerged in the water towards its tail end. He looked closer, seeing a small alcove under the bridge filled with tiny movements. This mother snake was protecting her young. She didn't move again, but was clearly aware of the woman who had interrupted her peace. Tiny black eyes were focused solely on Dani, and Valerio felt his chest tighten at the sight of her fear.

'Do you think you can swim to the edge?' He spoke softly, ready to move if the snake did. Judging by its size, it was one of the island's native boa constrictors—non-venomous, but who knew how it might react if it sensed a threat?

Dani laughed—a panicked, breathy sound. 'I can't move at all. I've tried.' She groaned. 'It's watching me.'

'Okay, I'll come and get you.' He pressed his lips together, stepping out of his shoes. 'It won't hurt you. The only poisonous snakes on this island are a lot smaller than this large lady.'

'Lady?' she squeaked, incredulous. '*I'm* a large lady—*that* is a gigantic reptile. Seriously, I'm in mortal danger here and you're being *respectful* of that thing?'

Valerio waded into the pool with slow, purposeful strokes. He reached her side in seconds, placing a finger against her lips. 'Careful. She might hear you and take offence.'

'Stop messing around.' She clutched at him, her hands shaking as she latched on to his wet shirt and folded her body against his.

He felt a low groan escape his lips as his body roared to life at the delicious contact.

'I'm sorry… Did I hurt you?' she breathed, her attention still largely focused on the snake.

Get it together, Valerio.

He sliced at the water to move them both closer to the edge. Now was definitely not the time to be losing his grip on his rediscovered libido. She was afraid, and she was trusting him to get her out of the pool safely, so he was going to do just that.

He began to lift her onto the lip of the pool, then instantly regretted it as she froze and clung to him even tighter. 'Don't *lift* me!' She pushed a hand at his chest.

Valerio growled with irritation. '*Dio*, again with the worrying. I have lifted you before and, believe me, I was not even slightly hampered by your size. You honestly have no idea how perfect these curves are.'

Her eyes went wide. 'I meant…don't lift me out where the snake can get me.' She began to blush a bright pink, her body suddenly softening in his arms. 'But…thank you.'

He froze for a long moment, just looking into her brown eyes, feeling her heartbeat thudding against his chest through the wet fabric of his shirt. He was an idiot. An absolute idiot.

His forehead dipped to press against hers as he fought the insane urge to kiss her. But he knew that if he kissed her now he would want more. He would want as much as he could have of her…as much as she was willing to give.

And where would that leave them? He had promised himself that the first time had been the last, that this was how it needed to be. And yet every time they were alone together it seemed like the most natural thing in the world to have her in his arms.

Thank God for the water around them, or she'd be all too aware of the nature of his thoughts.

'Valerio…'

She shifted against him, her thighs tightening on his hips as she tilted her face slightly. Her lips brushed against his, soft and wet, and he felt the ravenous beast within him roar with triumph. Surely, if she was starting it, it would be rude to stop her?

His arms banded around her, pulling her chest flush against him as he plundered her mouth, deep and hard. He felt her nails on his back as she moved against him, heard the sound of her groans as he pushed her back against the side of the pool.

With one hand he gripped her hair, tilting her head back and gaining deeper access, deeper control of the kiss. The darker forces in his mind screamed at him to take her right here in the water and to hell with the consequences. But it seemed Dani had different ideas. She stiffened in his arms, pushing him away with surprising force.

'I'm sorry...' he began, readying himself for the inevitable argument.

'No, Valerio... The snake moved again. I heard a splash.'

He turned, and sure enough, the reptile was now fully submerged in the water. He lifted Dani up with ease, doing his best to ignore the deliciously wet curves under his hands. Once he'd lifted himself out too, they both looked down at the impossibly long, dark shape in the water.

'I'll call Animal Control in the morning. Our snake friend has a nest of babies under that bridge that need to be taken somewhere a little bit safer.'

Dani shivered at the word 'babies', stepping backwards, away from the pool. 'I swear, I'll never swim peacefully again.'

That made two of them, he thought wryly, but for entirely different reasons.

The cool evening breeze cut uncomfortably through the wet fabric of his clothes. He needed a hot shower and a lot of distance between them to get his head in order.

Making a snap decision, he pulled off his soaked shirt and hung it over a chair, doing the same with his trousers. The outside shower was tucked into a wall on the terrace of the villa. It was fully stocked with toiletries and had a cabinet filled with towels. It seemed the rental company had thought of almost everything—except checking for hidden families of snakes, of course.

When he emerged from the shower, he hoped Dani would have gone inside. But she sat waiting for him on a sun lounger, with a towel wrapped around her body. A wet pile of fabric lay on the ground beside her. Her discarded bikini.

Valerio gritted his teeth, wishing he had taken his shower inside and then locked himself in his bedroom. Being a coward was infinitely preferable to this kind of sexual torture. If she had any idea what her mere presence was doing to him, with her damp curls hanging over her bare shoulders and the way she watched him through her lashes with a look of uncertainty on her beautiful face...

He tightened his fists, searching for control, hating it that she made him ache for all that he couldn't have. And he was finally admitting to himself that he did want to have her—not just because of sexual frustration or circumstance. He wanted *her*.

'You said you were sorry.' She spoke softly,

standing up to face him. 'About that kiss. But I'm the one who kissed you this time. I didn't even ask. Surely I'm the one who should be apologising.'

'You don't need to apologise. I'm the one who needs to apologise. My behaviour towards you has been unacceptable from the moment I came home,' he said, cursing himself as her eyes widened and she took a step towards him.

He raised a hand between them, holding her at arm's length.

'I'm sorry for how I spoke to you last night. I'm sorry I can't be…what you need. But we both know why we need to keep things professional here. My priority is keeping you safe, and that includes keeping you safe from me too. You've seen the way I am. I can't even be woken from sleep without becoming a danger.'

'That's ridiculous. You would never hurt me, Valerio.'

'You have no idea who I am. Not any more,' he rasped, his eyes lowering to take in the towel she clutched to her chest. 'I'm the man who promised to keep his best friend's sister safe. Then kissed her for the first time in front of an audience and had to stop himself from lifting her up like some kind of brute and carrying her off to the nearest bed. And if there hadn't been a damn snake in that pool, the same thing would have happened ten minutes ago. I have no control over myself around you.'

'Well…that would have certainly got everyone's attention…'

'This isn't a game any more. In two days you are going to be my wife…' He swallowed hard, trying to ignore the way her eyes darkened to deep burnished amber in the low glow of the setting sun. 'But I'm going to find the people behind all this, and once I'm sure you're safe—'

'What, Valerio?' She spoke quietly. 'You'll leave again? What a surprise.'

'I'll have our marriage annulled and you can get on with your life.'

'What life? I've spent the past two years working myself to the bone.' She ran a hand through her curls, taking a few steps away from him to compose herself. 'At least with you I feel…'

'What do you feel?' he asked, feeling himself itching to move closer, to coax this fire between them until it burned them both.

'I don't know…' Dani began, twisting the white towel in her hands, suddenly unable to look at him as she spoke.

Was she really going to be honest? She had kept her feelings for Valerio Marchesi under lock and key for so long it would be no effort at all to lie and agree to his sensible plans for their sensible marriage of convenience.

But she was tired of being sensible. She was tired of putting on a show of being strong and self-contained all the time.

'I don't think I have ever heard you speak in so many unfinished sentences,' he said.

'You said that I have no idea who you are any more,' she said, standing up and looking down at him. 'I think we're both different people now. Changed people because of events that neither of us had any control over. We've both been alone and we've learned how to cope with the unknown in our own way. I don't want to be alone any more, Valerio.'

He looked up at her. 'You're not alone. I'm here with you.'

'You're not,' she said quietly, feeling her bravado falter slightly but pushing on. 'Not really. And if I marry you, that means sharing a home with you, sharing my entire life with you... I can't be around you all the time in these intimate situations and not be affected. I'm just not that good an actress.'

'Are you saying you don't want to be around me?' He raised a brow.

'I do,' she said quickly, looking down at the ground and cursing herself for how badly she

was getting her point across. 'God, I really do...
That's the problem.'

Valerio stood up, closing the gap between
them with a single step. 'We're not just talking
about marriage any more, are we?'

'Look... I understand that this has never been
something you wanted.' Dani spoke fast, praying she wouldn't lose her nerve. 'But I need
to be honest. I'm really attracted to you. More
than I've ever been to anyone else. It's quite inconvenient, considering that we're planning a
marriage built on nothing more than business
and friendship, but... I just wanted to have that
out in the open.'

His fingers pressed against her lips, silencing her. 'Are you proposing to amend the terms
of our contract, Miss Avelar?' He wrapped his
hand around the towel, pulling her towards him
until they stood chest to chest. 'How much more
do you want?'

'I don't know,' she said breathlessly. 'How
much are you willing to give?'

He answered her with his lips on hers, his
hands spanning her waist and pulling her against
him—hard. '*Dio*, I thought I was already crazy
with wanting to have you. But now...with this
mixture of pretty blushing and the throwing
around of business terms...'

His lips trailed down her neck, his hands sliding down to cup her bottom through the towel. Dani moaned low in her throat, the power of speech slowly leaving her.

'Do you want me to make love to you, Daniela?' he whispered next to her ear, his hands kneading her skin gently.

'Yes… God, yes.'

He pulled back, an expression of awe on his face as he cupped her jaw and looked deep into her eyes. 'This will complicate things.'

'Only if we let it.' Her voice shook as she spoke. 'We're both adults. We know what this is.'

'I don't have any protection.' His brow furrowed, his hands tightening on her as though he feared his words might make her run away. 'I haven't been with anyone since before Brazil, and I don't really go around carrying condoms in my wallet. But I've had my yearly check-up since and I know I'm clean.'

'Me too—and I've had an IUD for years.' She pressed her hand to his cheek, hardly believing they were having this conversation. 'I don't want to think about this as a complication. I don't want to *think*, Valerio. I just want to do what feels right.'

CHAPTER EIGHT

HIS EYES DARKENED, his hand moving to the front of the towel, spreading over it slightly. His fingers trailed over the bare skin of her stomach. 'Tell me...does this feel right?'

She answered with a moan.

He continued his exploration, his touch sending her skin into an explosion of sensation. Her legs felt weak as he reached the edge of the bikini bottoms she had yet to remove, smoothing his hand down over her sex through the thin, still damp fabric. She bit down hard on her lower lip, tilting her head back as he licked a path of fire along the side of her neck.

She had never enjoyed sex in the past—she'd always been so consumed by her negative body image and her pesky inability to reach an orgasm. But her mind seemed unable to worry about that now, as he slid his fingers under the fabric and along the slick seam between her thighs.

'How about this?' he murmured softly against her skin, his teeth nipping at the area just below her ear.

Her answer was incoherent as she clung to him while he performed some kind of magic with his fingers. She had never felt such intensity from a simple touch before. Every slide of his hand sent fresh waves of pleasure shooting up her spine and down her legs.

Soon she was moving against him, powerless not to join his sensual rhythm. Her eyes widened in disbelief as she felt herself tightening around his fingers. The shock momentarily stopped her rhythm, her legs shaking beneath her as her mind got in the way of her pleasure.

'Do you want me to make you come, Dani?' he purred next to her ear.

'It's okay. I don't usually…' she breathed, her chest tightening. 'I mean, I've only ever been able to do it a few times by myself. And it takes far too long.'

Valerio pressed his forehead against her temple. '*Dio*, that image…you touching yourself… But right now I'm the one in control.' He continued to move his fingers in slow circles as he spoke softly in her ear. 'You're going to relax and come for me…right here. I won't stop until you do.'

Dani felt a breathless laugh in her throat at

the thought that this arrogant man believed he could simply will her to orgasm. But, God, she loved it. This artful combination of being commanded and cared for so thoroughly…it was almost too much for her to take. Her body seemed to relax just with his sensual presence.

She shook wildly at the lazy thrust and curl of his touch, feeling the pressure within her rise once again. This time she didn't fight it, and she listened helplessly as he whispered all the things he planned to do to her, letting his words add fuel to the fire that was already burning in her, wildly out of control.

When the wave of pleasure finally reached an earth-shattering climax, she could do nothing but hold on to him as the waves took her again and again. The intensity of the orgasm was too much, and she buried her face against his shoulder, his name falling from her lips like a prayer. Still he kept it going, only slowing down as she shook and fell slowly back to earth.

'I think I've proved your theory incorrect.'

Valerio bit his lower lip as he took in the rosy flush of Dani's cheeks and the delicious pout of her lips.

'I can't even think straight.' She smiled, half hiding her face against his shoulder.

'I don't plan to stop until you've lost the ability to speak.'

He fought the edge of his control as he took her by the hand and guided her back inside the villa, stopping to light two of the lamps on the bedroom wall. Letting go of her hand, he sat on the edge of the bed, looking up to take in the beautiful silhouette of the woman in front of him.

This was a bad idea—she had said it herself. But he no longer remembered any of the reasons why. Nothing mattered any more other than having her body under his and taking the entire night to explore every inch of her silky caramel skin.

She stepped towards him, dropping the towel from the tight clutch of her hands, baring her body to him. *Dio*, he had never seen anything as erotic as the sight of her blushing. Her hands flexed as though she wanted to cover her breasts, then dropped slowly down to her sides.

He remembered her words from before—her belief that she was somehow less feminine because of her size and her competitive streak. Less desirable because she was so unlike most of the women in her social circles. She had no idea how much she had tortured him with this delectable body for years...sitting across a boardroom table in her smart skirts, commanding the room with her brilliance.

This powerful woman actually doubted her beauty. Doubted herself in the bedroom because of some unqualified idiot in her past.

He bit his lower lip, anger and desire making his pulse pound in his veins. He would make it his personal mission to ensure she never doubted a single thing about herself again.

'Come here,' he rasped, gripping her hips and guiding her to straddle his lap.

Her breasts were the perfect size for his hands. He took his time, trailing his lips and tongue across one delicate dusky nipple before moving to pay equal attention to its twin. The soft moans that escaped her throat made him so hard it took all his willpower not to just do away with the idea of going slowly. The thought of burying himself inside her made him feel primal…on the verge of losing his mind completely.

But if this kind of sensual control and skill was all he had to offer her, then he was damn sure that he would prove his worth. He thrust out his hips, his erection straining against the front of his towel. Dani gasped, her eyes darkening as she followed his rhythm, grinding against him. She moved like a dancer, her hips rolling effortlessly in time with his. *Dio*, it felt so right, having her against him.

Then she stopped her movements, bracing one hand against his chest. 'Lie back.'

'I was wondering when you would start fighting me,' he breathed, following her command without question.

He lay back on the bed, raising both arms over his head in a display of submission. He watched as she positioned herself at his knees, untying his towel and pulling it away inch by agonising inch. She worked slowly, deliberately drawing out her movements as she bared him. Her hair brushed over the skin of his thighs and abdomen as she ran one finger down past his navel. His manhood pulsed, straining towards her touch.

'I've never done this before, either,' she admitted huskily, meeting his gaze with no embarrassment, just trust. 'Tell me if I'm doing it wrong.'

'*Tesoro*, I don't think you realise how effortlessly sensual you are…'

He breathed the words as she freed him and ran her fingers over his hard length. He closed his eyes for a moment as the tip of her tongue moved against him in slow exploration as she figured it out for herself. Opening his eyes against a wave of pleasure, he looked down to see her taking him all the way past her full lips, his girth disappearing into the molten heat of her mouth.

There was no way he would withstand this kind of pleasure for very long without bringing things to a very abrupt ending.

He thought about it as he watched her take him, and he imagined letting her bring him to release right here. The image sent an electric pulse up his spine, but he sat up, cupping her cheek with one hand and drawing her up along his body until she lay flush against him.

'I wasn't finished.' She smiled that slightly awkward smile he had come to recognise as a sign of nerves.

'I promise to have you in that exact position again before tonight is over, but right now it's taking all my control not to end this before we've even begun.'

Her eyes widened with understanding, a smug smile spreading across her lips as she lowered herself down to kiss him. Valerio took advantage of her position, pulling her close before rolling them over on the soft pillows so that she lay in the cage of his arms.

'My turn.'

He moved down the sun-darkened valley of her breasts, following the path of her ribcage until he reached the gentle curve of her stomach. She writhed with every touch against her skin, her honest reaction to his kisses sending him back to the brink of release once again.

'Tell me what you're thinking about,' he growled against the silky skin of her upper thigh. And then with both hands he spread her legs wide, settling his shoulders between them.

'I've…fantasised about you doing this…'

Her words came quietly from above him, spurring him on as he dropped featherlight kisses against the neatly trimmed downy curls that covered her. God, but she was perfect here too. She writhed, moving her hips against his mouth, begging him to stop his sensual torture.

He barely touched her for a few moments more, then surprised her by spreading her wide and moving his tongue directly against her in one slow stroke. She went wild, a sharp curse escaping her lips.

'Are you going to come for me again?' he murmured huskily against her skin.

'I can't…' she breathed, her head moving against the pillow with each stroke. 'Oh, God, stop—it's too much.'

He paused, only to have her hands grip his hair, as if begging him to keep going. Valerio smiled against her as he continued to stroke, again and again, keeping a smooth, firm rhythm. But the power he felt in bringing her to this point of madness was too much—he needed to have her soon.

She gasped in shock, beginning to approach another climax under his tongue, and he wasted no time in moving over her, spreading her legs wide and looking into her eyes as he entered her in one hard, urgent thrust.

He needed to be inside her as she came apart more than he needed to breathe. The time for taking it slow had passed, and he had burned out every last scrap of his control. He felt her inner muscles continue to tighten around him, heard her breaths coming in short gasps as she met the strength of his thrusts. She pulled his face down to her own, crushing her mouth against his so sweetly as her climax hit. And Valerio felt his own pleasure reach an unbearable peak, felt fire spreading up his spine and consuming him. He closed his eyes, pressing his forehead to hers as he came apart, joining her in mind-less oblivion.

Dani stared out at the hazy darkness of the moonlit night spilling in through the open terrace doors. Valerio's gentle snores sounded in the bed behind her. He had fallen asleep after another round of intense, earth-shattering sex. But she lay awake, wondering what would happen once he woke up and properly talked about what they'd just done.

She was afraid to move, as his arm was draped over her, pulling her tight to his chest. And something within her ached at the wonderful feeling of being in the cradle of his strong arms, even knowing it was only temporary.

She sighed. If she could just stay in this bed for ever she might imagine that things had deepened between them. If they never had to leave this magical island they wouldn't have to confront the reality that they shared a company together. That this was an arrangement, not a love match. That, while he was apparently attracted to her on a physical level, he would probably never feel even a fraction of what she felt for him.

She paused. What exactly *was* it that she felt for him?

Frowning, Dani slipped gently free of his embrace. Sitting on the side of the bed, she looked down at the strong profile of the man who was soon to be her husband. The engagement ring on her finger felt heavier than ever, its cool metal shining in the light of the moon.

She had agreed to live with him, share her life with him and trust him to keep her safe from the unseen danger that was closing in. But what were they to one another without this arrangement? Would he ever have fallen into bed with her if he hadn't been facing possible years of celibacy as her convenient husband?

Cradling her face in her hands, she breathed deep and tried to calm the anxiety within her. She was about to *marry* him—she couldn't have this many complicated feelings warring within her. She was falling into dangerous waters and it was clear she would be the only one hurt when it eventually came to an end.

She needed to keep her feet firmly on land— starting right now. Sleeping together in one bed seemed a step beyond sharing the occasional romp in the sheets, so surely leaving now would be a firm message to show she wasn't getting the wrong idea from what they'd done?

She stood up, pulling the comforter from the edge of the bed, and walked to the door, turning back just once more to look down at Valerio's sleeping form. She could do this—she could have what she wanted of him and still keep herself above water.

She went into her room and stepped straight into a hot shower, feeling the spray hit muscles that she hadn't used in years. She lathered soap across her skin, feeling her body tighten at the sensation, imagining it was Valerio's hands touching her, caressing her…

God, she'd had him three times and already she was fantasising about the next time.

Resting her forehead against the cool tiles, she breathed in deeply, calming her racing heartbeat. She sent up a silent prayer that she wasn't in completely over her head. They could mix a little pleasure into their arrangement and not risk ruining everything, couldn't they?

Before she could finish that thought, the shower door slid open and Valerio's broad naked form appeared through the steam as if in slow motion. The man was built like a prize fighter, and the shadow on his jawline made him look rough and dangerous. He didn't speak— just pulled her into his arms and kissed her as though he were a drowning man and she was his first gasp of air.

His hands tangled in her wet hair as the spray of hot water cascaded over them both. Framing her face in his hands, he looked down into her eyes, a wicked smile on his sinfully full lips. 'You left before I was done with you.'

'I'm just… I have no idea what this means. Us being together. I needed some space to think.' She met his eyes, feeling her heart still beating so hard she thought it might explode from her chest. 'What are we doing?'

'I have no idea, but I can't seem to stop.'

Dani felt her mind go blank as Valerio moved

closer, kissing her worries away. There was comfort in knowing that he was just as powerless against this insane lust. She would worry about the consequences tomorrow. Tonight she would just live in the moment. In this perfect moment with him, with the steam of the water surrounding them, slickening their skin as the heat rose even higher.

He stopped for a moment, his eyes serious as he looked deeply into hers. 'How on earth did you ever think you were bad at this?'

Dani felt a blush creep up her cheeks. 'Um… let's just say when it comes to sex, it's the one area where I've never been an overachiever.'

He pressed the length of his erection against her, leaning down to nip gently at the sensitive skin of her collarbone. 'I strongly disagree, Miss Avelar. You're a natural.'

'Well, you're the first guy to ever get me to… to finish the race.'

He bit his lip, and something deep and dark glittered in his eyes. 'Look at me. And if some idiot in your past told you it was a race, then he was playing the wrong sport.'

He dropped down onto his knees before her, framing her thighs with his strong hands. She shivered as his lips touched her upper thigh and began to kiss inwards.

'You should have been given more than a

thousand orgasms by now. You've been robbed of years of pleasure,' he growled. 'I plan to set that right.'

Dani closed her eyes, trying to remain upright as he kept his promise again and again.

CHAPTER NINE

DANI AWOKE TO the sun streaming through the terrace doors and the glorious scent of coffee teasing her nostrils from somewhere in the distance. She sat up, momentarily disorientated as she looked around at her unfamiliar surroundings. It felt like a dream that she'd spent half the night experiencing the kind of orgasms and intense sexual chemistry she'd only ever read about in the books she'd devoured in her college dormitory. She'd never believed it could ever be for her.

Every encounter with Kitt, her ex, had been prearranged—no surprises. Even down to the type of underwear she had worn. Comparing her ex to Valerio now, after last night, was like looking at discount price wine after drinking a vintage reserve Chianti. It left a sour taste in her mouth and she knew she was worth more. But of course Valerio wasn't truly hers. He was just acting the part.

She quickly shut off her ridiculous thoughts with a bracing shower, throwing on her silk robe while she applied various beauty products and let her curls air-dry. She'd promised not to do any work, but nabbed her phone from the nightstand, telling herself she would just take five minutes to check the most important emails.

Twenty minutes later she was engrossed in a text conversation with an insanely curious Hermione when Valerio appeared beside her and snatched the device from her fingers.

'I was in the middle of reading something,' she squeaked, jumping up to grab the phone back—only to have him hold it further out of reach.

'You are technically on vacation, Miss Avelar.' He tilted his head to one side, lazily looking down over her scantily clad body. 'I'm demanding that you actually take the day off.'

'I can't just switch off like that. There are things I need to check on with the new plans… things that need my attention even while I'm relaxing.'

'So you don't trust the relevant teams to perform their jobs?'

She huffed out a breath, knowing he was right. She was checking on them for the simple reason that she wanted to. She couldn't let go of the relentless force telling her to keep on top of everything, to make sure nothing was missed.

'Well, since you can't control yourself, I'm cutting you off.' He smirked, tucking her phone into his back pocket. 'If you want this back, you're gonna have to work for it.'

She felt heat creep up her spine at his words, her nipples instantly peaking at the suggestion he'd created in her mind.

He raised a brow at her, evidently noticing her physical reaction. Suddenly shy, she closed her robe a little tighter and turned around in a pretence of opening up her small case and organising her clothes. When she looked back, a shadow had crossed his features, but he quickly disguised it with an easy smile.

'Get dressed quickly. We leave in fifteen minutes.'

'Leave…for where?'

She froze in the middle of selecting a T-shirt. His eyes twinkled with the kind of mischief she hadn't seen on his face in years. He was up to something, and it made her both nervous and strangely excited.

'We're going on an adventure. I plan to make a pirate of you yet.'

Valerio was stubbornly silent as he waited for her at the end of the wooden deck, and only gestured for her to follow him down the rocky steps in the cliff face towards the tiny bay below. He carried a small bag over his shoulder and stopped occasionally to help her down as the steps began to grow steep.

He tried and failed not to be distracted by how carefree she looked in simple knee-length capris and a tank top. She hadn't got a scrap of make-up on and her curls were tied back from her face with a colourful silk scarf she'd found in one of the kitchen drawers.

He'd been unsure of what she was thinking from the moment they'd spoken that morning, so he was glad he'd arranged today's trip before the events of last night.

It sounded so simple…calling it 'the events'. As if it was a small blip they could just forget about and move on from. But maybe that was what she wanted?

The thought caught him unaware, making him almost miss his footing on the steps.

She'd been skittish around him all morning—maybe she was having second thoughts? Surely if that was the case he should be relieved. And yet the thought of her drawing a line under whatever this was before he was ready made something tighten in his gut.

It was simply pride, he assured himself. No

man wanted to feel rejected—especially not by the woman they were about to marry.

They emerged through the foliage onto the most beautiful little pebbled beach. The gentle curve of the land had created a perfect shallow pool where they could see tiny fish swimming.

Valerio gestured towards the end of the inlet, where a small wooden dock had been erected. The dock housed a single sleek black speedboat. 'I had this skippered over from the marina— figured I'd take a chance while we're here to get up to speed on our latest toys.'

'Oh, I see how this is. You get to do some work but I'm not allowed to?' she jibed, accepting his hand as she stepped down into the boat.

'This has never been work to me.' Valerio inhaled deeply as he fired up the engine and set his hands firmly on the wheel. '*Dio*, I forgot how good this feels.'

She sat back, watching the waves while he focused on pulling out from the small dock and gathering speed as they moved out onto open water. The boat was effortlessly smooth, and Valerio knew he was an expert at the helm. The familiar feeling that he had every time he was out on the water washed over him. It was as though he had finally come home.

He'd always had this affinity with the sea, this soul-deep connection. It was the thing that had bonded him and Duarte—their passion for sailing and exploring the world without fear.

Something within him stilled as he realised he had barely given his best friend a thought since the night before. Perhaps it was just the natural evolution of grief—the intensity of the pain wasn't any less but the frequency was bound to change and lessen. Guilt threatened, but he pushed it away, refusing to sully what he'd shared with Dani. He refused to mark it as wrong, somehow, when it was possibly the most right he had felt in a long time.

'Where are we going?' Dani moved to sit beside him, speaking loudly above the noise of the speedboat crashing its way through the waves.

'You'll find out soon enough.' He smiled, his hands moving to take hers and place them on the helm. 'But for now it's time to ease you into your new life as an explorer. Step one: you will now captain this boat.'

She shook her head. 'No! I've never had the first idea how to drive one of these things. Take it back.'

She squeaked as he took a step away, leaving her alone and holding on for dear life.

'Just relax and feel the power in your hands. Feel the hull slice through each well.' He spoke next to her ear. 'Keep your eyes straight ahead.

Brace your body and move with the water. Don't fight the current... Ease against it.'

Impulsively, he gently kneaded the tension in her shoulders. 'You're fighting it, Daniela. Breathe in deep and exhale... Lean into it.'

She rolled her eyes, doing as she was told, loosening her grip and easing forward. Her resulting smile was dazzling as she moved the boat over the swell without any tensing at all.

'Careful, now—I might start to think you're enjoying yourself,' he teased.

'I'm just very eager to earn that phone back.'

She pursed her lips against another smile as his hands covered hers on the wheel, joining her as they navigated over the water together.

Valerio had congratulated himself on his innovative idea of getting Dani to drive the speedboat to their surprise diving lesson excursion in Rodney Bay. But once he'd achieved the task of getting her out in the open water with their instructor, she had asked a million questions. The man had explained that this kind of diving was called Snuba—a cross between snorkelling and scuba diving—and that they would be connected to a small raft by air lines and safety lanyards the entire time.

Valerio tried not to laugh as Dani finally finished wrestling with the large diving mask on her face and took a long look at the depth of the water before them.

There was no certification required, because it was quite safe, but Dani still looked terrified now, as she stared down over the side of the boat.

Valerio advanced on her, his own mask making his voice sound muffled. 'We can just go back to the marina if you want?'

As he'd expected, she narrowed her eyes on him in challenge and turned to the instructor as he finished securing her weight belt, regulator and air line to the small safety raft. But as she moved to ease down the metal ladder on the side of the boat, her foot slid and she tumbled rather ungracefully sideways into the sea.

Valerio felt a shout leave his throat, moving to dive in after her, but the diving instructor stopped him with a hand on his chest, showing him he had a firm grip on her safety harness.

Sure enough, Dani emerged instantly and grabbed on to the large blue-and-white water tank floating beside the boat, pulling the regulator from her mouth and letting out a strangled cough that Valerio felt deep in his chest. He watched with awe as she gasped, holding on to the safety lanyard as she tried to adjust the mask on her face and remove the water.

'See, I'm a natural!' she shouted nervously.

'Well, Marchesi, are you coming in, or are you having second thoughts?'

Valerio finished his own set-up and eased down the ladder. They followed the guide's instructions, paddling out a specific distance from the boat before preparing to dive down. It had been a long time since his own deep-water scuba diving days, but he still felt the thrill of being out in the depths, with nothing below them but glittering blue adventure, pass through him.

He had only dived down about a metre when he looked to his side and realised Dani hadn't come with him. Using his own natural buoyancy, he kicked his way back up to where she still clutched tightly to the safety lanyard on the raft.

'Okay, so I was bluffing. You go ahead. I'll just watch from here!' She spoke over the noise of the waves.

'What about adventure?' He popped his own regulator out and pushed his mask up on his forehead, looking into her eyes. 'What about trusting me?'

'I do trust you. We both know that *you* can do this. You've always been brave and fearless. So don't let me hold you back. Go…please.'

'While you just wait around up here in the safe zone? Is that it?' He hardened his gaze.

'And how much happiness has *that* got you so far, Dani? All that fear and tiptoeing around... not taking any risks.'

'It's kept me alive, hasn't it?' she retorted, then gasped at the realisation of what she'd said, shaking her head. 'I'm going back to the boat. I'm sorry.'

'Look at me.'

He pulled her towards him, the water lapping at them on a light current. He could see the instructor watching from a short distance away. He didn't care—he wasn't letting her go without saying what he needed to say.

'There's a difference between actually feeling alive and just going through the motions of life. This, right here, being so far out of your comfort zone, is where you'll find the former.'

'What would you know? You've practically been a ghost for six months. Are you telling me that *you* feel alive?'

He took the hit of her words, knowing they were the truth. 'I deserve that. But the truth is I forgot how this felt—how healing it is to let yourself just be free. These past few days you've brought a part of me back to life that I'd thought lost for ever. I just want the chance to push you to do the same. The way I should have done the first time you asked for my help.'

She frowned, her bottom lip quivering

slightly. For a moment he worried that he'd gone too far and opened too many old wounds. A part of him hoped that she would just swim away from him—that was what he deserved. Maybe it was just too little, too late, as the old saying went.

But, as usual, this woman had far more strength than anyone gave her credit for. She steeled her shoulders, taking one hand off the raft and extending it to him. 'I'll need your help. I'm shaking too hard to let go.'

For a moment Valerio stared down at her hand, shocked at such an open show of vulnerability and trust. Then, once she had the regulator in her mouth, he grabbed hold of her, feeling the tremors in her fingers vibrating against his own. He grasped her tightly, embracing her for a long moment as he pulled her bodily from the raft.

She stiffened, then moved with him, following his guidance as they trod water together in an easy rhythm. Valerio locked his eyes with hers, gesturing with the fingers on his free hand as he silently counted down from five and they slowly dropped below the surface together, hand in hand.

Daniela remembered, as a child, running after her brother through the gardens of their country home and always stopping the moment she got as far as the black gate that led into what Duarte had christened 'the haunted forest'. It had been just a normal country wood, but the trees had been so dense it was almost pitch-dark once you were a few steps in.

Her brother would assure her it was okay, but her fear would always stop her from stepping nearer the shadows and into the unknown beyond. She'd needed to see safety ahead—not jump in and think later, the way he had.

Now, even as an adult, she trod softly and kept to her plans. She was fearless in the boardroom, and fearless in what she wanted for her career, but deep down she sometimes felt that she was still that child, staring at the line between safety and the unknown and keeping herself stubbornly behind that line.

But once she'd emerged from the water with Valerio's hand still in hers, she'd finally had a taste of what it was that pushed him to test his boundaries the way he did.

Pushing past her own fear had been terrifying, but that fear had got less and less as she'd dropped down into the ocean and seen the wonders that lay below the surface. Schools of tiny, vibrant coloured fish had danced through the current, and as Valerio had guided her deeper, she'd been entranced by the play of light on the seabed. She'd watched tiny creatures as they scuttled in between rocks and coral, and had spotted a couple of spiny lobsters locking claws with one another. The highlight of the dive had been the moment a sea turtle had swum nearby, its graceful body turning in the water and reflecting glorious beams of turquoise and blue light.

Dani had been utterly charmed by the world below the surface, filled with such simple quiet wonders. Wonders that she would never have seen from her spot on that life raft. She was grateful that Valerio had pushed her. Clearly he had seen something missing in her life—something she had never known she needed. And he was right. This feeling of adrenaline and triumph was healing.

She felt free. She felt as if she could take on the whole world.

The feeling carried on for the rest of the afternoon as, back on the speedboat, Valerio unveiled a small picnic lunch which he'd had delivered from a local restaurant. She knew he was still worried about her safety, and was thankful for the time he was giving them alone together, without their security detail.

Valerio took them out to a remote spot along the coast of Rodney Bay, from where they could view the impressive length of Pigeon Island in the distance. The food was from one of the finest chefs on the island: a delicious spread of green figs and fresh lobster, followed by a dessert of banana cake—a special St Lucian recipe that was deliciously spiced and sweet.

They talked for what felt like hours and she remembered exactly why she had always liked talking to him. He didn't just listen and nod; he gave his full focus to her—just like with everything he did.

She found herself telling him how she'd been relieved to cancel her plans for her own firm and how fear had always held her back. He seemed surprised at first, then quietly pensive as he listened to her ramble.

For the first time ever, she admitted out loud that it had been a need for comfort and closeness and safety that had driven her to work at Velamar after her parents had died. Then, when success had come upon her, she'd found excuses to not run on ahead into the unknown. She had held on tight to her position at Velamar, holding herself back by only taking on short-term outside contracts.

In turn, he told her of his decision to drop out of college and how disappointed his parents had been—how he had almost gone back just to please them. But he had known he would never have been happy in the perfect corporate tower with his perfect brother, as much as he wished he could have been. There had always been something wild in him—something that needed the open sea and the pull of adventure.

Sailing had always been his first love, so he'd bought his first yacht, and the tabloids' 'Playboy Pirate' had been born—a result of uncertainty and youthful pride.

A companionable silence fell between them and Dani realised that she'd always known there must be a lot more to Valerio Marchesi than anyone saw. He wasn't just the party-mad reprobate the media painted him as. Perhaps on some level he had purposely harnessed that image as a means to control his fall from the supposed grace of the Marchesi dynasty—to defend himself from the possibility of failure. It was strangely comforting to think that perhaps she wasn't completely alone in her fears.

Dani watched as Valerio began to pack away the remains of their food and tried not to focus on the swirl of emotions warring inside her. She was grateful to him for giving her this perfect day, but it wasn't gratitude that had her skin heating as he lay back on the blanket and let out a deep sigh of satisfaction.

They hadn't really talked about the night before and what it meant. Suddenly she found herself wondering if maybe he wanted to draw a line and leave it as a one-night stand. It would be understandable, considering the complications that carrying on would mean. But seriously...how was she ever going to look at him again without remembering all the things they'd done?

His body was an impossible distraction. He already looked more tanned and vital after only a few hours in the strong afternoon sunshine, and the pale blue linen shirt he wore only served to draw more attention to the impressive power of his shoulders and biceps. A memory of having those arms around her the night before rose up, her skin tingling with an electric current as she forced herself to look away.

'You have the most expressive features—did you know that?' He spoke softly, with a smile in his voice. 'What were you thinking just now?'

Dani looked back to see his sunglasses were off and the sun and sea were reflected in his cobalt-blue eyes. She cleared her throat, finding her mind blank and all her snappy retorts having deserted her. This man made her brain malfunction. She should be furious—should use that anger to stop herself from diving into this crazy fire that felt as if it was just waiting to explode between them again at any moment.

They were going to be married, for goodness' sake. This inconvenient attraction was fast turning into something deeper. The man was a drug—one taste and she couldn't think of anything but her next hit. But she couldn't torture herself like this. That way lay only danger and pain.

She bit her bottom lip, standing up and climbing down to the cockpit to grab a bottle of water in a vain effort to cool herself down. She heard him approach from behind.

'I told myself I'd let you lead the way—but, *Dio*, Daniela… I want to kiss you again.' He spoke softly. 'I haven't been able to think of anything else all day. Have you forgotten so easily?'

Her breath was shaky as she braced her hands on the smooth surface in front of her. 'I don't think I'll ever forget…but we both know this is a bad idea, Valerio.'

Warmth pressed against her from behind… the barest touch of strong, calloused fingers on her hips through the fabric of her dress. She closed her eyes, preparing herself to turn round and tell him that they had to be sensible. Then his lips traced featherlight kisses along her nape and she felt her traitorous body leap to attention. She pressed back against him, feeling him hard and aching, exactly the same way she felt deep inside.

She turned in his arms, her mouth finding

his like a homing beacon, needing to taste him, needing all of him.

After a minute they were both frantic with need and tearing at one another's clothing. Her brief, momentary panic at being out in the open, where anyone could sail past and see them, was quickly overcome by his wicked whispers to enjoy the risk. So she did.

She leaned back against the side of the boat, spreading herself wide for him, letting him know that she was his for the taking. She was *all* his.

His guttural groan was almost enough to push her over the edge as he grasped both her thighs, his fingers like a brand on her skin as he forced her even wider to accept his length. His love-making was primal, and frantic with longing, as though he too felt as if at any moment one of them would come to their senses and bring things to a halt.

She felt the swaying movement of the boat underneath them as he thrust hard and fast, taking her closer and closer to heaven. As she came, she looked up at the sky and let out a sound of pure abandon, not caring who heard her.

After a second, slower exploration of one another, Valerio helped her back into her clothes and insisted she sail them back to the small dock at the villa. His powerful body behind her guided her the whole way. And as she helped him gather their things and finish docking, she felt laughter bubbling in her throat at the fact that not only had she sailed a boat and deep-dived off one in a single day, she had also had two very public orgasms on it too.

'Something funny?' He raised a brow, offering her his hand as she stepped off the wooden pier onto the soft pebbles of the beach.

She smiled. 'I can't remember the last time I just felt...happy.'

'I'll never look at that boat again without remembering you, spread out against the mahogany deck with the glow of another orgasm on your skin.' He pulled her close. 'How many is that now? Not nearly enough yet.'

His use of the word 'yet' seemed to break a spell of sorts. It seemed that both of them had remembered there was a time limit on whatever it was that they were doing. She bit back the words on her tongue—the urge to ask him when it would be enough. When it would be over.

They both knew that there was no room for casual sex in their arrangement, that they had to get a handle on this. Besides, she wasn't sure 'casual' even began to describe the need she felt when he touched her.

She had agreed to share a home with him

when they got back to Europe—but to sleep in a bed alone, knowing he was separated from her by only a thin wall. She shut her eyes against that unwelcome reminder of reality.

'I'm not ready for today to be over yet,' she whispered against his chest as she listened to the sound of the waves crashing against the pebbles on the shoreline.

'Who said it was over?' Valerio smiled. 'You may have tackled your fear of open water, but you have far from learned your lesson about pleasure.'

'I'm pretty sure I have bite marks on my neck that contradict that statement.' She laughed as they began the tortuous climb back up the cliff steps to the villa.

'Not all pleasure is sex, Daniela,' he scolded, his eyes wicked and full of mischief.

He smiled down at her as they reached the top step, then turned to look up at the house— and his entire body suddenly froze.

Dani bumped straight into his muscular back, clinging to the material of his shirt to stop herself from toppling backwards, down the way they'd come. 'Valerio, what on earth—?'

She gasped out the breath she'd sucked in, and then followed his narrowed gaze to see a small gathering of people on the upper deck, peering down at them with interest.

'Is that your brother up there?' Dani spotted Rigo Marchesi, smiling down at them, and by his side she was pretty sure were Valerio's mother and father.

Valerio cursed something in fierce Italian under his breath, gripping her hand tighter and hauling her up by his side. 'We might have to hold off on the pleasure. It appears that my family have invited themselves to our wedding.'

CHAPTER TEN

IT TRANSPIRED THAT his family, namely his mother, had arrived to perform an intervention of sorts.

Valerio held his annoyance in check by a thin thread, his gaze anxiously seeking out his fiancée throughout dinner as she was practically interrogated over their sudden alliance and why they'd selfishly kept it hidden for so long. He felt the tension building between his brows as he watched his mother and sister-in-law fawn over Dani's engagement ring at the opposite end of the table. The three women had barely stopped talking—and his mother was asking question after question about what exactly they'd planned for the wedding. He had been a fool to think that Renata Marchesi would pass up the chance to be mother of the groom a second time.

His father had been his usual reserved self throughout dinner so far, but Valerio's brother, Rigo, had more than made up for it with his subtle ribbing about how relaxed and well-rested Valerio looked.

'I hope we haven't interrupted anything here between you and your fiancée?' Rigo said now, raising one dark brow as he took a sip of red wine.

'Should your wife be flying all this way at this stage in her pregnancy?' Valerio changed the subject swiftly.

'She's still in her second trimester. We decided to have the older girls minded and treat ourselves to a romantic weekend before the baby arrives.' Rigo raised his glass to his wife, meeting her eyes across the table for one heated moment.

Valerio cleared his throat pointedly. 'A pity you couldn't have taken your romantic weekend somewhere else, rather than ruining my private elopement,' Valerio said, feeling a strange mixture of discomfort and awe at the fact his family had taken the time to fly all this way.

Nicole Marchesi stood up and moved to take the seat beside her husband. 'Dani's friend Hermione has already told us the truth about your trip here.'

Dani froze at the end of the table. 'Hermione has spoken to you?'

'She styled our wedding years ago, and we've

kept in touch. She's horrified about the whole thing. Really, Valerio, I can't believe you.'

Valerio felt heat creep up the back of his neck. 'You don't understand the whole situation, and I didn't want to worry you.'

'I understand very well.' His mother stood up, censure in her tone. 'Romantic elopement? You didn't even book a proper venue to say your vows, for goodness' sake. It's a disgrace!'

'Papà thinks you've got your fiancée pregnant.' Rigo's eyes twinkled.

Valerio exhaled slowly and saw Dani's shoulders drop with relief. Her friend clearly hadn't told his family the whole story—just enough to ensure this intervention of sorts.

'I know my son.' Renata turned to Dani, shaking her head. 'He's an impulsive fool, which might seem romantic right now, but he doesn't think things through. *Per l'amore di Dio*, I don't care if she's pregnant or not. You're on one of the most romantic islands in the world and you were going to get married in a courthouse?'

Valerio had tensed at the word 'impulsive', hating it that his family fully expected him to be running off for a shotgun wedding. Clearly they still painted him as a wild fool. But they knew nothing of his life—only what he allowed them to see.

'Daniela is not pregnant. We were just trying to keep things small and intimate.'

He groaned inwardly, knowing that calculating look in his mother's eyes all too well. She wasn't deliberately trying to be unkind. She was big on creating memories, ensuring beautiful moments were made at important events. To Renata Marchesi, very little would seem more important than ensuring her second son got married in a way that befitted their family name.

'Small and intimate?' She nodded. 'I can do that. Just give me twenty-four hours.'

As his brother let out a bark of laughter, Valerio pinched the bridge of his nose between his fingers. He should have expected this. His parents' wedding was still talked about and they had been married for thirty-five years. They had stood together to watch their oldest son say his vows in a spectacular ceremony at a French chateau, and were now feeling the joy of welcoming grandchildren into their growing family.

How could he tell them that he didn't want an audience for what was only going to be a short-lived venture—another perceived failure to add to his ever-growing list? He couldn't tell them about the nature of his marriage to Dani without revealing the danger she was in. Maybe some day he would tell them the truth, but right now he had no choice but to go along with the charade.

The evening wound down in companionable conversation, with Rigo taking a moment apart from the others to quietly update him on the plans he'd put in place to tie up Daniela's inheritance and ask what progress had been made on the investigation.

After a while they joined the women on the terrace, and Valerio was once again drawn back into the charade of normal family life. He rested his arm across Dani's shoulders, feeling her settle her weight against him.

Across the table, Nicole announced that the baby had started kicking that week. Dani's eyes lit up with wonder as she asked if it hurt, at which Renata laughed and said that some day soon she might find out for herself.

He felt her tense against him, moving away ever so subtly. Dani's withdrawal got under his skin for some reason. As did the way his brother interacted so easily with his family, making jokes and talking about plans to build a tree house during the summer.

He had never before been jealous of the pressure Rigo had been put under as heir to the Marchesi fortune. But right now, seeing his brother rest his hand possessively across his wife's stomach, he felt an uncomfortable tightening in his chest. Needing to excuse himself, he stood and moved inside the house.

In the master bathroom, he splashed cold water on his face and glowered into the mirror. *Get it together, Marchesi.*

Dani appeared in the doorway behind him, her eyes filled with concern. God, she was so beautiful. It almost hurt to look at her without touching her. He wanted to take her, to consume her until the emptiness inside him was full of her laughter and her brilliance.

It was hard not to feel as if he was using her like a drug when the effect of just being in her company was so addictive. And it wasn't just the sex, either. He enjoyed being with her... found himself looking for ways to make her smile. What was happening to him? They had agreed on a time limit for whatever this thing was between them. And neither of them was interested in risking their business partnership over a fling. And it *was* just a fling.

A fling that was about to escalate into a marriage.

Valerio turned around and leaned back against the vanity unit. She didn't move closer and he told himself he was relieved. If his face showed anything of the chaos of emotions warring inside him, she would probably turn around and call off the whole wedding.

She *should* call it off. She deserved so much better than this. She deserved more than a brief few days of hot sex with a man who didn't come close to deserving her. She deserved the wedding of her dreams with a good man who was reliable and logical and safe—everything he could never be for her. And this fictional perfect husband would make her happy—he would be with her as she carried their perfect children and lived her life in blissful happiness.

Valerio was shocked at the swift kick of jealousy in his gut.

'You left the table so suddenly I was worried.' She stepped forward, reaching out to touch his arm in a soft caress. 'What's wrong?'

Her gentle touch was more than he could process. The pressure in his forehead was close to the breaking point and he couldn't seem to gather his thoughts.

'You shouldn't have followed me.'

Even as he said the words, he knew he didn't mean them. He knew he wanted nothing more than for her to keep looking at him that way, caring about him.

A look of uncertainty flashed in her beautiful eyes and she quickly removed her hand. 'I'll get back to the others, then.'

'I'm fine.'

He turned away from her, splashing water over his face again and avoiding her burning gaze.

'Before I go, I want to talk to you about this whole ceremony thing.' Dani cleared her throat to try to stop the sudden shake in her voice. 'The flowers…the violin players…'

'My mother enjoys making an occasion of things, and I can't deny her after the year she's had. I hope that's okay?'

He was watching her reflection in the mirror, clearly waiting until she nodded.

'They're all expecting to see a happy couple saying their vows, so that is what we will give them. We have no other choice.'

Dani felt his words hit her somewhere in the chest with all the subtlety of a sledgehammer on porcelain. She had followed him expecting him to have been set a little off balance by this sudden seismic shift in their plans. But this… It was as if shutters had come down over his eyes, blocking her out.

Confusion mixed with hurt, and anger rose briefly, before she shut them down tight and stretched her lips into a smile.

'If anything, it will add to the authenticity of the whole thing,' she said, and a breathless ghost of a laugh escaped her lips, seeming to bounce off the bathroom walls, mocking her. 'I'm a little jealous that I didn't think of it, to be honest.'

He turned around and stared at her, a muscle in his jaw beginning to tic rather menacingly. She waited for him to speak, in her own foolish mind still clinging on to a thread of hope that he might have something good to say. Something that wasn't about the coldness in his eyes, the detachment.

'We have no other choice,' he'd said. As if he'd already been forcing himself to do this and now it was becoming an unbearable spectacle.

The fact that she had felt so connected to him for a moment just now only served to cheapen things further, making her feel weak and used even though he'd made it quite clear where he stood when it came to any feelings between them.

She felt the shameful threat of tears building in her eyes and turned quickly towards the door.

'Dani, wait.'

She turned back, swallowing hard past the lump in her throat and pasting on another bright smile. 'Yes?'

'I… I just wanted to say that I don't regret this weekend,' he said stiffly, his expression hard and intense. 'I don't regret whatever this was between us.'

'Neither do I.' She smiled—as though her

heart *wasn't* breaking into a thousand tiny pieces at his use of the past tense. 'It was…exactly what I needed. Thank you.'

She turned away again before she completely lost her composure and moved to close the door softly behind her. She wasn't prepared for him to barge through it, bearing down on her in the hallway.

'"*Thank you*"?' he growled quietly, eyes glinting like sapphires in the evening light.

'What do you *want* me to say?' She felt her head shaking, her insides trembling dangerously. She needed to get away from him—get some breathing room before she totally embarrassed herself.

'I didn't do this as some sort of *service*, if that's what you're telling yourself.' His voice was low and gravelly, his eyes refusing to leave hers. 'The marriage is one thing, but let there be no misunderstanding that this…whatever this energy is between you and I…was just for us.'

'Valerio…' She bit her lip as he moved towards her and flattened his hands against the wall on either side of her head.

'Tell me you don't want me,' he whispered. 'Even just one more time.'

'Why don't you tell me what it is that *you* want, Valerio?'

She heard the longing in her voice. Felt the

choking fear of this coming to an end and the foolish desire for him to offer her everything she dreamed of. She didn't just want one more time. She couldn't bear the idea of accepting whatever little offering he wanted to give to get her out of his system and move on to someone else. She wanted it all and it terrified her.

'Right now? I just want you to kiss me,' he murmured huskily.

She reached up, her lips seeking his. Her hands dug into his hair and pulled him close. The growl he let out in his throat sent heat flooding straight to her groin. God, would he ever stop setting her off like this?

But he had never given any indication that he thought of this as anything more. He remained rooted firmly in the present, refusing to think ahead, to see the risks. She couldn't ignore the red flags any longer—she couldn't place all her faith in blind hope. She was no longer just falling into dangerous territory with this powerful, fierce warrior of a man. She had plummeted right into the unknown.

She was in love with him.

She broke the kiss, closing her eyes tight against the realisation, her throat convulsing wildly as his breath fanned her cheek. His delicious scent was everywhere, his warm body so close, and she could feel his eyes on her. But she had a feeling that even if he wasn't right there she would still feel him. He had climbed his way into her chest, folding himself around her heart.

What had she got herself into?

'Are you crying?' He held her chin, tilting up her face with a deep frown.

She swiped the tears from her face, forcing herself to meet his eyes even as she felt her heart break. 'Valerio…let's not make this harder than it needs to be. I don't think either of us are ready for the fallout. I think…this needs to end now. While we can still go back to being friends and partners in this arrangement.'

Footsteps sounded in the hallway, and without warning, Valerio's mother advanced on them, a phone hooked in between her ear and her shoulder. Dani scrambled to rub the moisture from her eyes and regain some composure.

'Daniela, I just wanted to check if you prefer white roses or…' Renata paused, taking in the sight of the two of them standing stiffly side by side.

Dani groaned inwardly, knowing her nose was likely bright pink and her feelings completely obvious. She prayed that the smile she forced would be convincing and mumbled something about adoring white roses before quickly excusing herself and going back into the bathroom.

She slid the lock closed before moving to the mirror and grabbing a wet flannel to scrub at the slightly smeared mascara under her eyes. Mortification crept up her chest and heated her cheeks.

Closing her eyes, she scrambled for her phone and hit the button to call Hermione, but was greeted by her friend's voicemail. She compensated by sending a single text, all in capital letters, asking what on earth she'd been thinking to tell Nicole about their elopement. No reply came.

Eventually she was going to have to leave this bathroom and face her fiancé. It was no big deal, she told herself, and straightened her shoulders and took a few deep breaths. She was in the business of presenting an image of what people wanted to see. She could do this—she could pretend to be his adoring fiancée for the rest of this trip. She could stand by Valerio's side and vow to love and cherish him as his wife without falling to pieces, couldn't she?

She sucked in a sharp breath. No big deal… No big deal at all.

CHAPTER ELEVEN

THERE WAS NO opportunity for Valerio to continue their conversation, as they weren't given any more time alone together. At the insistence of Renata, the men were hurried away to stay in one of the new yachts on the marina for the night, while the women stayed at the villa.

Valerio had explained the heightened security presence as his own need for protection, which his family had accepted with a slight look of worry. In the short time since Dani had come crashing back into his life, he had almost forgotten that the world still presumed him mad with paranoia.

Now Valerio stood alone on the bow of Velamar's brand-new luxury mega-yacht and tried to ignore the sense of restlessness that had hounded him since leaving Dani at the villa. His father and his brother had gone ahead to create an impromptu bachelor party, promising that it wouldn't involve anything inappropriate but that he would need his wits about him.

Valerio looked at his watch. He had another five minutes before they expected him to follow. He guessed it would involve gambling of some sort. His father was an avid poker player and was known for his skill. He sighed. Even the thought of a night of mindless gambling wasn't enough to calm the irritation brought by how badly he had handled things earlier.

She had *thanked* him for bedding her, as if he had been doing her a service. As though he had been trying to assuage his guilt by giving her orgasms as penance? His jaw tightened with anger at how little she must think of herself if she believed such utter nonsense. There was nothing charitable about his behaviour towards her.

If he'd been a better man, he would have kept his attraction under control. He wouldn't have complicated their arrangement and risked the fragile friendship they had formed. He had played with fire and ignited a full-blown blaze. He should be thankful that she'd seen sense and ended things.

But even now being away from her felt wrong, somehow, even though he knew she wasn't any safer with him by her side. He had left his two best security men with strict instructions to ensure she was completely secure. He had finalised all the necessary arrangements for the surprise he'd planned for her tomorrow. He'd wanted to see her face when she saw it, but it was probably better if he kept his distance until the ceremony. He wished they hadn't had that argument…that his family hadn't arrived and set off all alarm bells in his mind.

But above all, he realised a part of him missed her, needed her company, as if they had spent years of this fragile new intimacy together—not just a few days.

He frowned at the thought. He *didn't* need her—he had always made sure he didn't need anyone. He was Mr No Strings. They had just both been celibate for a long time, so it was only natural that it would add to the kind of explosive sexual chemistry they had… It was a recipe for this addictive feeling. But he was not going to become hooked. They'd had one amazing weekend of blowing off some steam and that was over.

Gritting his teeth, he closed his eyes and focused on the sound of the sea lapping against the stern to try to unwind the tension in his gut. Maybe having his family here planning this wedding had got under his skin? There was no other explanation for the crazy thoughts he had been entertaining since he'd left the villa.

He knew that someone like him could never have the kind of stable, normal lifestyle his father and brother enjoyed. It was utterly ridiculous. Did he actually think he could give a woman like Dani the life she deserved?

He had already resigned himself to being alone until he found out who was behind Duarte's murder. He hadn't thought further beyond that. It was hard enough just getting through each day with his rigid handle on his PTSD intact. He was broken. His body and mind had been damaged and scarred and, no matter how hard he tried, he would always have to bear the reminders of what had happened in Brazil—a catastrophic event that he had caused by being his usual impulsive, reckless self.

His head security guard appeared, snapping him out of his thoughts. 'Mr Marchesi, there's a man here to see you. Says it's urgent.'

It was his private investigator from Rio, Juan, his face looking entirely the worse for wear and his clothes dishevelled.

'You didn't answer my calls, so I put a flight on your tab.' He stepped forward, placing a tablet computer in his hands. 'You can thank me later.'

The man sank down onto a nearby lounger as Valerio's eyes scanned the file, seeing Angelus Fiero's name. He felt anger begin to surge within him, expecting the worst. But the contents of the report were so far from what he'd expected that he found himself needing to sit down.

'Get me Fiero on the phone—now.' His voice was a dry rasp.

'He's currently in an operating theatre after sustaining a gunshot wound.' Juan sat forward. 'He'll survive. He went after them himself, it seems. The politician who ordered the kidnapping is dead and all evidence of the blackmail material he'd been keeping about Duarte has been destroyed, thanks to Fiero's clever manoeuvrings over the past few weeks. I believe the threat to Miss Avelar has been neutralised.'

Valerio felt the air leave his lungs. Angelus Fiero had been on their side all along. 'How do we know there aren't still others who are waiting to take over? How do I know she isn't still in danger?'

'Fiero has used his intel to turn the tables on a few other corrupt individuals linked to the Brazilian government. He's had the Avelar land and properties in Brazil made untouchable. They can only be used for charity, so they're worthless to any other money-grabbing corrupt developers now. As is every other piece of her inheritance. She's safe. I'm sure of it.'

Valerio nodded slowly, wondering why he didn't feel a sense of elation at the news.

He thanked Juan, and instructed his security guard to ensure that the PI was paid handsomely for his efforts. Alone again, he debated heading straight over to the villa and telling Dani the news. Telling her everything. But it was late… and he didn't want his mother to overhear their conversation.

Renata Marchesi was going to be upset enough at the cancellation of her dream island wedding ceremony. Because if there was no longer a threat, there was no longer any need for a wedding. He could tell his family what had happened—why he had been so secretive. Maybe one day they would all look back on this and laugh.

They would have made one another miserable anyway…he and Dani. But, then again, maybe they might have found some way to be happy in their arrangement…

He stood still for a long time in the dark, staring out at the inky black waves as he imagined what his life might have looked like if things had been different.

After a fitful night of sleep, alone in the bed that still smelled like Valerio, Dani barely registered the conversation at the breakfast table. It was dawn, and the whole house was buzzing with activity in preparation for the wedding. Renata and Nicole were talking about the details of the ceremony planned for that evening—a sunset wedding, followed by an intimate family dinner prepared by a world-famous chef who lived on the island.

The moment she was able to, she slipped away and wandered out onto the deck, staring at the glorious sunrise as it kissed pink and orange along the waves and wondering how on earth she had managed to get herself into such a mess. It was her wedding day and she was utterly miserable. If she'd been the brave, fearless type, she would have just run away. She almost smiled, imagining herself commandeering Valerio's boat and sailing towards the horizon.

Heels tapped across the deck towards her and she inhaled, turning and preparing herself to tell even more lies to this wonderful family who had made her feel so accepted.

But it wasn't Renata or Nicole who stood in front of her.

'Jeez, this place is locked up tighter than a prison.' Hermione smirked. 'I had to show my ID and video-call your fiancé just to get his goons to let me past the gates.'

Dani's mind had barely recognised her best friend's smiling face before she launched herself full force into Hermione's arms. It was as though all the pressures of the day had been released, and she did nothing but hold her tight for a long time.

When they finally separated, she took a step back and lightly punched Hermione in the bicep.

'Hey, is that how you thank me for blowing off a job with royalty to come and be your maid of honour?'

'I wasn't planning to have an elaborate wedding at all until *you* intervened!' Dani said under her breath. 'His family aren't supposed to know anything about what's really going on here.'

'By that you mean the fact that you're having hot sex with your soon-to-be husband?' Hermione said dryly. 'That's utterly scandalous, Dani. How will they ever recover?'

Dani suddenly regretted the instant messages she'd been firing back and forth with her best friend. 'Be serious. It's not a real marriage— none of this is real—and it's only going to hurt them once they find out it's all lies.'

'*Is* it all lies, though?' Hermione asked softly. 'Because the look on your face in that picture you sent me of you two out on the boat… It's the first time I've seen you look happy in a long time. Does he make you happy?'

Dani swallowed hard, turning around to hide

the sudden flood of wetness to her eyes. Yes, he made her happy. He made her feel stronger than she'd thought she was capable of being. He made her feel beautiful and powerful and utterly devastated all in the space of one day. He made her feel far too much for it not to be utterly catastrophic to her soul once he eventually walked away. Because he didn't feel anything for her other than a fleeting physical attraction and a responsibility to keep her safe.

'Dani...' Hermione spoke softly, laying a hand on her shoulder. 'Did I mess up here? I just thought of the wedding you lost out on before, and the awfulness of the past few years, and I wanted something beautiful for you.'

Silence fell between them. Then Dani exhaled a slow, shaking breath and turned to press her face into her friend's shoulder. 'Thank you. I'm really glad you're here now.'

They were interrupted by the arrival of Renata and Nicole, holding champagne glasses. Sharing a pointed look with Hermione, she joined their toast to a beautiful wedding and a happy marriage to follow.

'I'm sorry now that I didn't buy a proper dress.' Dani frowned, realising for the first time that the simple beige linen dress she'd packed was really not going to be appropriate any longer. She watched as the three women exchanged a look of pure mischief, and then Hermione leaned towards Dani's future mother-in-law and whispered in her ear.

'I asked these ladies to wait until I got here to surprise you,' Hermione said, and smiled, pulling her by the hand towards the house.

Dani followed Hermione upstairs to the master bedroom—Valerio's bedroom. At some point it had been filled with boxes of flowers and small bags bearing designer labels. Hanging on the frame of the four-poster bed was a large white garment bag.

Dani felt time stop as Hermione slid the zip downwards and revealed the most spectacular blush-coloured gown she had ever set eyes on. It was the dress Dani had pointed out to her friend at a fashion week over a year ago, when she had confessed that her ex had influenced the choice of her first traditional white wedding gown, which she'd had to embarrassingly return when he jilted her.

Hermione had been outraged, but had never brought up the conversation again. Clearly she had not forgotten.

In a blur, Dani was undressed and zipped into the gown, awed at how it fitted perfectly to her body like a second skin and flowed in all the right places.

'You remembered… How did you get this?'

she breathed slowly, her hands stroking the material with awe. It was the same one. There was no doubting it. Even down to the hand-sewn rose-shaped gathering on the bodice.

'Your fiancé called my office yesterday, the moment he realised the wedding was going to be more than a simple affair. He asked me to choose the perfect dress as a wedding gift—and to bring myself, of course.' Hermione moved beside her, tipping her face up and wiping away a small errant tear that had slipped out. 'This is a *real* wedding, Dani. You both just haven't realised it yet.'

Dani thought of Valerio's thoughtfulness in helping her tackle her fear of the ocean. The way he'd held her as he told her how beautiful she was. The way he'd looked into her eyes as they made love. The sense of overwhelming rightness between them.

Now she was being told that he had gone so far as to make sure she had her best friend here, to obtain her dream dress… It was more than anyone had ever done for her before… It was too much.

She was overcome with the need to know what it all meant. What they meant to one another.

'I need to go to him.' She turned to Hermione and saw her friend's eyes light up with glee.

'There's no way I can marry him without laying everything out on the table, consequences be damned. I'm done with being afraid.'

'I like this change in you.' Hermione hugged her close. 'And I hope that man knows how lucky he is.'

They both knew there was no way Renata would allow Dani to leave without asking a million questions and worrying, so Hermione offered to spin a story and cause a distraction while Dani slipped away.

She briefly considered the speedboat, and a dramatic exit, but she wasn't quite that adventurous yet. So she walked up the driveway to the small hut that housed the two security guards and turned on her best smile, matched with her most authoritative tone. She didn't have time for any of their safety protocol nonsense.

'I need to see your boss. Right now.'

Valerio had just stepped out of the shower when he heard the door to the master cabin burst open. Like something from a dream, Dani walked into the bathroom, her eyes filled with blazing emotion.

'You're wearing the dress…' His voice was somewhere between disbelief and wonder, and a part of him was cursing fate for throwing this vision at him when he had been preparing to go to her and call off their entire wedding. 'Why are you here?'

'I had a whole speech planned on the drive over...' Her voice shook as she looked down and realised he only wore a towel. 'Oh, God... I should go.'

Valerio gripped her wrist and pulled her back towards him. 'Don't.'

She moved closer to him, her eyes filled with a look that both terrified and delighted him. A look he had no right to see. She needed to know all the facts. She needed to know that she didn't have to trust him or rely on him any longer. That she didn't need him.

'I need to talk to you before...' She paused, one hand reaching out to lay against his bare chest. 'Before we go ahead with this.'

'I need to talk to you too.' He inhaled deeply, glad that they were alone for this moment. That he could give her privacy, away from prying eyes and ears.

'I lied,' she said suddenly. 'I don't want things to end. The thought of not being with you again is unbearable.'

With disbelief and shock, he pulled her closer until they stood chest to chest. 'I've hardly been able to stop thinking of this...of what you do to me. It's like I have no control when it comes to you.'

'Me too.'

Her voice was a husky whisper as she pressed herself to him, her eyes widening as she brushed against the hard ridge of his erection. The look of instant heat she gave him was enough to bring him close to the edge as his lips lowered to hers in a fury of urgent need and frustration.

The sound she made against his mouth was half surprise and half seductive whimper as she slowly melted against him. His hands cupped the delicious curve of her behind, grinding her against the unbearable hardness that ached to be inside her.

Dani felt the urgency in him like a rising tide as he walked her backwards until she was pressed against the cool tiled walls. His eyes glimmered with intent as he slowly raised the full skirt of her wedding dress up her thighs. The material was light, and easily folded around her waist. She worried for a split second about crushing the fabric, but then decided it would be fine.

He moved to touch her, to feel how slick and hot and ready she was for him. His eyes darkened to the colour of a raging storm.

Her white lace underwear refused to stay to one side, and he let out a low growl, tearing at one side and throwing the scrap of lace to the floor. She bit her lower lip, feeling a thrill go through her at such a primal display. His lips nuzzled against her neck, biting softly.

'*Dio*... I need to be inside you right now.'

'Yes...' she breathed, feeling his hands grip the curve of one thigh and lift it so she was spread wide for him.

He dropped his towel and slid into her easily, her body singing out in sweet relief at being filled with such perfect hard heat. His thrusts were demanding, but his rhythm was just what she needed—she needed to feel that warm tension building deep inside her.

Every hard stroke brought her higher, and she clamped a hand over her mouth as she fought not to moan. They were far enough away from anyone else on the yacht not to truly risk being caught, but the thrill of it only added to her arousal.

Without warning, he gripped her other thigh and lifted her against the wall for even deeper access. She stiffened and tried to stop him. He shut off her protests with his mouth, the urgency in his body telling her he was far from burdened by her size. He pulled at one strap of her dress with his teeth, freeing one dark nipple above the fabric and taking it greedily into his mouth.

With his head bent low she could clearly see the reflection of him taking her in the mirror on the opposite wall. He followed her gaze, his eyes wicked as sin as he quickened his pace, giving no mercy as he took her over and over until she cried out against her hand.

'Just look at you,' he growled, his eyes almost reverent. 'Do you see how beautiful you are?'

She looked at the flush on her cheeks as she felt pleasure mounting, at the plump swollen flesh of her lips. She looked like a stranger.

She felt utterly weightless in his arms as she rode out her climax, feeling it crest and take her like a rush of electricity until her entire body shook. He was right there with her. A few hard thrusts and he came hard inside her, his head tilted back and eyes closed tight as though he were in pain.

After a moment he stepped back and grabbed a towel from the rack, wetting it and kneeling down to cleanse her. The movement was so caring she felt her throat clench. He didn't meet her eyes, however, as he stood up and put himself to rights. Then he reached down to grab her torn underwear from the floor and stared at it with such ferocity that she inhaled a sharp breath.

'I didn't mean for that to happen.'

He spoke with his jaw tight, and there was a sudden tension in him that made Dani feel the need to reassure him.

'Well… That's not exactly what I came here

for, either.' She forced a small laugh, still slightly out of breath as she pulled her dress down.

'What *did* you come here for, then?' he asked roughly. 'Because I was just on my way to see you.'

She tried not to read into his words, into his implication that sex was all they had. Even though he had told her that was all he was capable of giving her. They'd agreed to end things, but here they were after ten seconds alone together, panting in the aftermath of what had possibly been the most intense lovemaking she'd experienced with him. That had to mean something, didn't it?

'I came here to say that I'm not going to marry you today without telling you how I really feel.' She inhaled once more, fighting the twist of anxiety in her stomach at the leap of faith she was about to take. 'I can't pretend to be your wife, Valerio. Because I'm in love with you, and the only way I'm marrying you today is if it's real.'

Silence stretched between them for a moment, and she felt her heartbeat racing wildly in her chest. She forced herself to stand tall and meet his eyes, knowing she owed herself this moment of risk. She knew she would never regret giving him her heart, even if he handed it right back and walked away.

'I don't want to be your wife in name only. I want it all. I want everything that you said you can never give me.'

'What if I told you there was no need for us to get married any more?' He spoke quietly, his eyes stubbornly refusing to meet hers.

'What do you mean?'

'The threat to you has been neutralised.'

'You should have come straight to tell me. How long were you planning to keep this to yourself?'

'My private investigator informed me late last night. I waited to confirm the details myself and it's true.'

He told her of Angelus Fiero's involvement, about the blackmail and the corrupt politician. He went on laying everything out on the table until his head hurt and she sagged back against the wall, her face filled with disbelief.

'You said you were coming to see me this morning,' she said. "Were you planning to call off the wedding?'

'Yes, of course,' he said quickly, then caught her sharp wince. 'I mean… I was going to tell you everything. We both agreed that this marriage was just for your protection, but now… there is no more danger. Does that not change things?'

She nodded once, her lips pressed into a thin

line. 'Of course… It changes everything. I just wish you'd told me before I came here.'

'Dani, wait.' He placed his arm on the wall to stop her leaving. 'I've told you who I am… I've told you that I'm not the right kind of guy for you. You need to go and find out who you are and what you want without the threat of danger influencing you.'

'Valerio. I just laid my entire heart on the line.' She flashed him a deep look of disdain. 'My feelings for you never depended on you being wrong or right for me. I accepted you for the man you are—not the one you think you should be.'

'I don't want to leave things like this.' He frowned, hating it that he was hurting her but knowing he had to let her go.

'If you don't have anything else to say, then I'm going to leave, before anyone sees me in this dress.'

She waited another moment, refusing to look up at him, before disappearing quickly through the doorway and out into the hall beyond.

He let her go, telling himself that it was better this way even as everything in him fought to follow her. As though distance might help, he launched himself into the first speedboat he could find in the yacht's docking bay, pushing the vessel to its limits, needing to feel the lightness that always came with being on the water.

The lightness didn't come.

After a while he gave up punishing the boat and cut the engine, bobbing in the open water as he watched the sun rise higher in the sky. He could be selfish, he thought. He could follow her and take all that precious love she'd offered for himself. He could pretend she wouldn't grow to hate him, even though everything in him knew she would. He wasn't built for the kind of love she needed.

She would move on from this and start anew...find someone better. As for him... He wasn't so changed that he would pine over a woman, was he? He cursed aloud, slamming his fist against the wheel. He couldn't feel any pain, but the awful emptiness in his chest was a different matter entirely.

CHAPTER TWELVE

THE AIR IN Rio de Janeiro was warm and heavy as Dani walked out of the airport and into a waiting car. Blissfully, the chauffeur was not eager for conversation, so she had plenty of time to rest her eyes and prepare herself for whatever lay ahead.

Heartbreak was just another inconvenience right now—along with Angelus Fiero, who had refused to stop calling her every day for the past week until she'd reluctantly agreed to book a flight to Rio and hear him out.

It wasn't that she didn't feel gratitude for the part the older man had played in bringing justice against those who had been responsible for so much pain and loss. But something about coming back to Brazil felt wrong, somehow.

It was as if she was adrift amongst the old shadows of a life and had no idea how to navigate. The last time she'd set foot in Rio, she'd had her parents and her brother by her side, her family unit intact. Memories of her childhood were just as foggy as the cloudy sky above, which threatened to spill with rain at any moment.

Dani frowned as her car came to a stop outside wrought-iron gates and looked up at the concrete façade of the Avelar family villa for the first time in over two decades. It seemed like a lifetime ago that her ten-year-old self had said goodbye to the palatial mansion just outside the city, as she was torn away from the only home she'd ever known and forced to start over in England.

Was it any wonder that she had clung to her twin amidst all the constant change in their lives over the past two decades?

As she stepped out into the warm afternoon and told the driver to wait, Valerio's words rang in her ears. *'You need to figure out who you are and what you really want.'* The trouble was, she *had* figured it out. She had told him exactly what she wanted and who she wanted.

The memory of Valerio's eyes before she'd walked away from him seemed like a dream. She shook her head. Had it really been a week since she'd seen him? It seemed as if only hours had passed since St Lucia. Since he'd held her hand as they dived into the depths of the ocean together…since he had looked into her eyes in

Monte Carlo after he had kissed her for the first time in front of all those people...since she'd felt the heat and power of his body as he'd turned the tables on her that first night and tied her to her own bed.

Anger fuelled her as she dug through her bag in search of the old brass key. She rubbed roughly at the space in the centre of her chest, refusing to give in to another bout of tears and self-pity. She had done enough of that in the days after she'd returned to London.

She'd left St Lucia a week ago, returning to her tidy white apartment in Kensington and immediately sending a formal letter announcing that she was completely removing herself as an active partner of Velamar. Valerio had not attempted to contact her, but she'd told herself she didn't care that he was glad she wouldn't be working alongside him. It was irrelevant, and it wouldn't change her own course of action in finally taking the plunge and launching her firm. She should have done it years ago.

It stung like a fresh wound, entering what had once been her family home now completely alone. The air was dry and utterly still inside, where white dust sheets covered furniture like old-movie-style ghosts. A shiver ran from the base of her neck down her spine. But she surprised herself with how boldly she stepped over the threshold and laid her bags on the floor.

A quick scan of the barren downstairs space had her chest tight with emotion, so she distracted herself by opening shutters and windows, bringing light and much-needed fresh air into the stagnant dark rooms.

When she next looked at her watch, she was shocked to see that almost an hour had passed. She was covered in dust, sweat glistening on her brow, but something warm and precious hummed within her that felt suspiciously like relief.

It had never sat well with her to leave this beautiful house closed up and vacant. Her parents would have been happy to see it being taken care of, to see their daughter reconnecting with her roots in the home that held such precious memories.

She cleaned herself up as best she could and then set out for the hospital, to find out what exactly it was that Angelus Fiero simply had to tell her in person.

Two hours later she finally emerged from Angelus Fiero's hospital bedside onto the street, her legs feeling as if they might give out at any moment. It turned out the man had a very pressing reason for bringing her here. One that involved a web of secrets and strategies that her brother himself had created. Once she was safely alone in the dark interior of the car, she fought the urge to give in to the hysteria and tears threatening to burst free from her chest as she processed everything the old man had revealed. But one fact shone out high above the others.

Her brother had survived.

Duarte was alive. He'd been recovering from severe brain trauma and was being kept in a secret location, but he was alive.

A thousand thoughts flew through her mind at once, but one drowned out all the others. She wished Valerio had been there with her for this. She wished she hadn't been alone to take the hit of a bombshell of this magnitude.

She was hardly aware of the drive back to Casa Avelar. Her brain was stuck somewhere between numb shock and trying to analyse what the logical next step might be. But there was nothing logical about any of this. Nothing at all.

Stepping out of the car, she paused as she noticed that the lights in the villa were all blazing bright and a sleek black car was parked at the top of the driveway. She paused on the stone steps, her senses on high alert. The front door opened and she felt the tightness in her chest released on a heavy exhalation of breath.

Valerio.

His shoulders filled the doorway, the light grey material of his silk shirt making him seem ethereal, as if she could reach out to touch him and he might not even be there.

'You didn't answer my calls.' His voice was low and effortlessly seductive, with just a little hesitance thrown in.

'So you flew to Rio? You could have just left a message with my PA.'

She fought the shiver that ran down her spine as he held her in place with that intense gaze. The look in his eyes startled her. It was how she imagined she must have looked every day for the past week.

Miserable.

She needed to tell him what she'd just found out—that her brother was still alive and had been kept hidden somewhere in Brazil. But a part of her wanted to know why he was here, how he felt about her, before he knew about Duarte.

Had he missed her?

The look in his eyes was almost enough to tip her over the edge of control and send her melting into a puddle at his feet. Was it simply regret at the loss of the precious friendship he'd spoken of? She held back, schooling her features as much as possible. Once burned, twice shy might not apply to every situation, but that didn't mean she should dive headfirst into this particular fire without thinking it through.

She crossed her arms and allowed the silence of the evening air to fall heavily between them. He moved first, taking a few steps down the gravel driveway with ease, showcasing long, powerful legs encased in worn designer denim. Of course he *would* look more delicious than ever, she groaned inwardly, imagining how awful she must look in comparison.

'I spoke to Angelus Fiero.' She tried to control the wavering of her voice, determined not to break down in front of him but desperately needing to unburden herself. 'He told me that Duarte is alive.'

Valerio froze. 'That's impossible. I saw him die.'

Dani opened her bag and handed him the folded hospital document as she relayed the information she'd been given of Duarte's injuries and rehabilitation in a facility deep in the rainforest.

For a long time Valerio just stared at the piece of paper in his hand.

'I thought about what I would say for the entire flight here…' He spoke softly, his hand moving for a moment as though he wanted to touch her but decided against it. 'I didn't plan on you telling me any of this. I'll come with you. We will find him together.'

Dani nodded thankfully, letting the silence pulse between them before she spoke. 'Valerio…why did you come if it wasn't to hear what Fiero had to say?'

Valerio hesitated, then seemed to make a snap decision. 'I came for you, Dani. I should have come sooner. I should have followed you the minute you left my yacht. I told myself I should be relieved that everything had changed, that you were free of needing me, but…' He shook his head, looking away from her.

Dani felt something in her heart stretch— something that felt foolishly like hope blossoming. 'You were scared,' she said softly, a thrill of electricity shooting through her when he looked up and met her eyes.

'I'm known for taking risks and following my instincts, even if it leads to trouble.' He shook his head. 'But the things I've done in the past… risking my safety and my wealth on crazy ventures… None of that scared me. I never truly valued my own life. I always saw myself as dispensable.'

She shook her head, ready to launch into a vehement protest, but he reached out a hand, stopping her.

'I thought that risking our friendship and disrespecting the promise I'd made to Duarte was what terrified me. But seeing this paper now... knowing he's alive out there somewhere... It doesn't change anything for me. We will deal with that as it comes.' He took a deep breath, laying the document down on the step behind him. 'Dani...look at me. I now know I was just afraid of what I felt—not the consequences or the risks. I don't need anyone's permission. Letting you move on without ever telling you how I feel is no longer an option.'

He laid his hand over hers, turning it to find she still wore the diamond engagement ring on her finger. She hadn't been able to part with it just yet. He looked down at her, meeting her eyes with such reverence that it took her breath away all over again.

'I think I've been slowly falling in love with you since we were teenagers and I didn't have a clue. So I ignored you—I ran away or I provoked you. I'm far from perfect, and I'll probably make mistakes, but I'm asking you for a second chance.'

She felt emotion clog her throat as she fought to formulate the words rushing through her head. In the end she just threw her arms around his neck, burying her face in his shoulder.

Eventually she leaned back, looking into his eyes and seeing the relief and emotion there.

'You put far too much effort into playing a part and worrying about what others think…but I see a man who is so much more than a playboy pirate. You put me first every single time, and I…' She felt her throat catch. 'You told me that if you want something you just have to take a deep breath and dive… So I knew that I couldn't walk away without telling you how I felt. Without telling you what you could have if you were only brave enough to take a risk of your own.'

He closed the small distance between them with lightning speed and pulled her up into a kiss that made her entire body shake with emotion. His hands entwined with hers, coming up to press against his thundering heartbeat.

Dani smiled against his lips as he devoured her. He kissed her until she was kissing him back with every ounce of love she had…until she felt the breath sigh from her and her entire body melt into his arms. Only then did he pause for breath, burying his face in her neck and exhaling on a deep, primal growl.

'Sorry, I'm not good with pretty words or speeches,' he said softly into her hair, his hands still clutching her tightly against him, as though he feared she might run away if he loosened his grip.

'That was pretty eloquent, I think.' She bit her bottom lip, feeling as if there was a hint of magic in the air—as if this couldn't be real, this perfect moment. But the smile that spread across his full lips mixed with a look of fierce possession told her everything she needed to know.

She gasped, looking down as he slid her engagement ring off her finger with one smooth movement. Silencing her with a finger on her lips, he took a step back and slowly lowered himself down to one knee.

'I know I've technically proposed already, but I feel the situation requires a do-over.' His eyes met hers with intense heat and emotion. '*Tesoro*... I want to be your husband and your partner. I want us to create a family and a life together. I swear I will spend the rest of my life giving you every single thing you desire if you'll have me.'

'I've never wanted anything as much as I want to be your wife for real. I love you. I want us to live together, work our crazy schedules around each other. I want to have your babies, Valerio Marchesi. I want all of it.'

She took a deep breath, fearing her heart might actually burst out of her chest with the effort of getting the words out. She felt shivers run down her spine as he slid the ring back onto her finger and stood up, pulling her into a tight embrace.

She felt a calm settle over her like nothing she'd ever experienced before. Despite the unknown of what might lie ahead of them, she knew he would be by her side. Together they would dive headfirst into whatever adventures lay ahead, and as long as she had her hand in his, she knew things would be okay.

EPILOGUE

THE NOVEMBER RAIN poured down on his face as Valerio raced across the busy rush hour streets, narrowly missing a black cab as he finally reached the door of the hospital. He barely stopped to announce himself at the desk, his breath crashing in and out of his lungs as he took the stairs two by two.

The prestigious London hospital was a maze of corridors as he passed by door after door, finally finding the one he was looking for. The one he'd been inside every day for the past week. He came to a stop inside the brightly lit room—only to see an empty bed, perfectly made up with white linen. Fear closed off his air supply for a long, panic-ridden moment, before a woman entered the room behind him, wearing bright blue scrubs and a white mask.

'Mr Marchesi, you're just in time. Your wife is in Theatre.'

He was rushed down to the emergency operating theatre and handed a bundle of scrubs to change into. His hands shook as he pushed open the door to the bright surgical space and saw Dani's beautiful face, white with fear, as she lay surrounded by doctors and nurses and the rhythmic beeping of medical equipment.

'Valerio!' Her shout of relief was palpable as she reached out to clutch at his sleeve and pull him close to her face. 'I can't believe this is happening. It's too early!'

Valerio steeled himself at the anguish in her voice and murmured words of encouragement in her ear, his hand gripping hers tightly as the surgeons performed their work on the other side of a blue screen.

It seemed as if hours passed before the doctors announced that the baby was out, then spent a while bending over Dani with furrowed brows. Moments later a loud, healthy infant's cry erupted in the room and he felt his shoulders sag with relief as he pressed his forehead to Dani's and let emotion take over.

After a flurry of movement and various checks, the doctor assured them that their daughter was perfectly healthy and didn't need any care other than her mother's skin.

A nurse placed the tiny form on Dani's chest and Valerio felt his heart swell with love and gratitude as they both cradled and stroked their child's glorious head of jet-black curls.

'What do you think Leandro will say when he finds out he got a baby sister instead of a brother?' Dani asked softly, her eyes filled with laughter.

Valerio winced, thinking of the serious-faced three-year-old at home in their town house, being spoiled by Nonna and Nonno Marchesi. Leandro had been quite clear that a baby brother was the only thing he would tolerate.

'I'm sure we'll figure out a way to bring him around,' he said, and smiled, leaning in to brush a kiss on his wife's forehead.

Once the surgical team had finished the after-care for her emergency caesarean procedure, Dani was returned to her comfortable private room, where she promptly fell asleep. She awoke a short while later, to the sight of her husband cradling their infant daughter in his strong arms.

She was quiet for a while as she watched them, her heart threatening to burst with joy and relief that they had been blessed with a healthy child for the second time.

Their firstborn son had been born exactly on his due date almost two years previously, on the day of their second wedding anniversary. Valerio had joked that he was just like his mother: shockingly efficient and punctual.

The comment had turned out to be quite accurate. Leandro *was* just like her and Duarte had been as children, in spirit and in looks—apart from the brilliant Marchesi blue eyes that accompanied his rather serious gaze. She thought of her twin brother, feeling an echo of that old sadness mixed with relief. Her relationship with her twin had been strained for a time once they'd found him and discovered the depths of his ordeal and the web of deception behind it. But now...now she could hardly believe her luck at having so much family around her.

'I'll have to tell Duarte he won our bet,' Valerio murmured, looking at their daughter. 'I thought we'd have all boys. This girl is definitely going to steal my heart.'

Dani laughed. 'What are we going to call her?'

'I was thinking... Lucia.' He turned brilliant cobalt eyes on her.

Instantly Dani's thoughts travelled back to the island where they had fallen in love, said their vows, and where they'd returned every single year since, to the villa they'd now bought together.

'Valerio...' She felt her throat close with emotion. 'That's perfect.'

'*She's* perfect. Just like her mother.'

He placed their daughter in her small crib, his movements careful and confident. She had almost forgotten how natural he was with babies. He had been the one to show her tricks to get Leandro to sleep for longer and to bring his wind up, while she had been a shivering mess of nerves for months.

She sighed and leaned back on the pillows. He moved to sit alongside her, being careful of her tender abdomen and the tubes still attached to her arms.

'I have never been more afraid than when I walked into that room today and saw an empty bed.' A frown marred his handsome brow as he looked down at her, stroking one hand across her cheek.

'I was terrified too, once I realised something was wrong and they wanted to get her out so suddenly. I was so worried that you wouldn't get here in time. But I swear I could hear my mother's voice in my head, telling me to breathe. And I knew that we would all get through it okay.'

'You were amazing. You are a goddess of a woman—have I told you that?' He leaned forward, his lips brushing across hers softly, one hand cradling her neck. 'Your strength never ceases to amaze me. How on earth did I get so lucky?'

'I love you so much,' she whispered against his lips. 'But all this sweet talk isn't going to make me want more babies.'

'You said the same after the first one.' He smiled, nuzzling her ear. 'But two is perfect for me. I think your staff will kill me if I keep getting you pregnant—that company of yours is skyrocketing and they need their fearless leader.'

'Motherhood only adds to my superpowers.'

Dani smiled, thinking of the perfect top-floor London offices of Avelar Inc.

She had done it all—her own company, her perfect home in the English countryside and her wonderful family. Valerio had promised he would give her everything and he'd stood by her every step of the way, giving her his full support as they juggled their work and home lives together as a team.

'Lucia Marchesi...' Dani smiled down at her sleeping daughter. 'I don't think the world could handle another Riviera pirate—especially if she looks anything like you.'

'If she's like me she'll need to find the right person to balance out her wild spirit.' He leaned back, draping an arm carefully over her shoulders and dropping a kiss on her collarbone.

Dani leaned back into the power of his embrace, letting out a soul-deep sigh of contentment and happiness. 'This is quite an adventure you've taken me on.'

'We've only just started, *tesoro*.'

* * * * *

Adored The Vows He Must Keep?
You'll be unable to resist the next story in
The Avelar Family Scandals duet,
coming soon.

And why not explore these other
Amanda Cinelli stories?

Resisting the Sicilian Playboy
The Secret to Marrying Marchesi
One Night with the Forbidden Princess
Claiming His Replacement Queen

Available now!